Beyond the Resurrection

Beyond the Resurrection

GORDON EKLUND

DOUBLEDAY & COMPANY, INC.

GARDEN CITY, NEW YORK

1973

First published in *Amazing Stories,*
April & June 1972, copyright 1972 by
Ultimate Publishing Co.

First Edition

ISBN: 0-385-06737-2
Library of Congress Catalog Card Number 72–84909
Copyright © 1973 by Gordon Eklund
All Rights Reserved
Printed in the United States of America

To Ted White

Contents

Beyond the Resurrection

First Day

CHAPTER 1

CHORUS:
Children of New Morning

Outside it continued to rain as it had rained unceasingly for the past twelve hours, but within the north wing of the student dormitory of New Morning school, fifty-eight children, who ranged in age from ten to thirteen years, chattered excitedly in quick, whispering voices that were sufficiently loud to be heard by their companions but not so loud as to attract the attention of either Him or Her (as they were called), the appointed checkers for the night, who prowled the outer corridor, wondering, *Now what are they up to? Are they sleeping? Are they talking?* The checkers, a man and a woman, both teachers, wished this part of the night were done, for it was always the worst, waiting for the children to slip into silence, and after that it was only staying awake, finding some way to pass the time, keeping the eyes open and alert, struggling toward dawn.

This was New Morning, a school, an experimental school, owned and operated by an aged, crinkled man named Joyce Larkin, a former Hollywood gossip columnist who had founded the school some thirty years ago, designed to turn out children who were both healthy and whole, located on the northwest corner of an island, and the island was located near the center of a narrow body of salt water known as Puget Sound (after the explorer Peter Puget), which was located in the state of Washington, United States of America. The time was near the turn of the century and it was not a good time for this place.

And the children? What good is a school without children,

and what point to having a dormitory without occupants? The children occupied the dormitory, both wings, including this one, the north wing. Right now they were talking. Talking, yes—but softly. The lights had darkened around them only a half hour earlier, and most were yet far from sleep. Outside, it continued to rain without pause.

Some of the children gossiped. They talked about the school, its founder and teachers. They talked about each other:

—And Sheridan, he says to me you'll either do it my way, young man, or you'll not do it at all, and, you know, he simply doesn't belong here. This isn't the place for Sheridan. I've tried to tell Larkin that. What's he doing with his you'll either do it my way or you'll not do it at all? What kind of freedom do you call that? And all I wanted was to cut the net off the old basketball hoop so I could use it for protection in a gladiator skirmish. What kind of freedom? I want to know. What kind of education?

Or:

—Beady-eyed Kenery looking at me through fruit pink eyeglasses and I walked right out on her and went down to see Larkin and I told him I wanted to go fishing and not listen to algebra, and he says he wants to know what I mean. And I tell him I want to be a fisherman when I get my certificate and I need the practice now if I don't want to starve then and he shakes his head and says for me to go down to the bridge. And I tell him there ain't a fish in the creek between here and the Sound, and he believes me, the dumb fart.

(And some of the children were dreaming, for some of the children, more withdrawn or introverted than the rest, perhaps less far along in their therapy, or perhaps not, they preferred to sleep rather than talk, and so they drifted, dreaming of distant wondrous marvels flowing beneath a bright noonday sun.)

Or (more gossip):

Two girls occupied the last bunk in the left-hand row here in the north wing, the first older girl stationed in the upper berth, and the second younger girl in the lower, but right now locked snugly together in the lower bunk, but only because it was so much easier to talk this way.

—She went with him. Look. She's gone (said the older girl).

—And him (said the younger, softly) and him, old August. It's raining piss too. Listen.

The rain pattered and danced against the distant wooden roof of the dormitory, striking softly and gently, for the rain of this northern country was a gentle rain, though often continuous, a rain of beauty and rebirth and not one of darkness or death. The two girls, one eleven and the other thirteen, had been friends for two years, much closer than the hypothetical sisters neither had known. Both had names, but the names don't matter.

—They'll get wet. Everytime August does it again, he'll think of the wet. I know. My first time was during a snowstorm.

—Mine on the beach.

—It was not. You've never done it. You can't. You're only eleven.

—I can too. And I did.

—When?

—But August. I can't even imagine it. Why would Melissa want to go with him? He seems so cockless, even if he must have one somewhere. He acts almost like he's never done it before, never even thought of doing it, and he's almost thirteen.

—He hasn't. He told her. I listened. He said he never felt the urge till tonight.

—And she went with him? Like that? Oh no.

—She wanted to. She's asked him before. I heard her. And she likes him. And she likes it. You know how she is about it.

—But Tallsman's checker tonight. He's a prude.

—Not him. His wife. Skinny wicked witch.

—Him too. If he catches them coming in all wet with their butts all soaked, he'll . . .

—He'll what? There's nothing. McGee is the other checker. She'll take care of him.

And: much much more. Gossip, talk, chatter, dreams, and the reflection of dreams.

And outside it was raining, the drops plunging against the squat green bush beside the rushing brown creek, washing away the accumulated dust of late summer, and below they crouched and waited. They were not talking. A boy and a girl. Neither much older than twelve or thirteen. Waiting. The rain had slipped lightly within their sanctuary, creeping beneath the bush, and their feet were slightly damp, their legs. The two of them.

—August?

—Yes, Melissa.

—Are you sure you want . . . ?

—Yes, I have to.

—And you don't mind?

—No, of course not.

—And you think you'll like it?

—I don't know. Can't we see?

CHAPTER 2

GREGORY TALLSMAN:
Can the Sun Shine Bright at Twelve Midnight?

Sitting. And reading. His eyes lifting and his eyes straying. Oh yawn; oh boredom; oh midnight. Gregory Tallsman turned his head slightly and peered at Corlin McGee. The two of them were sitting together on a wooden bench in a white corridor beside a high wooden door. Corlin was reading a book. She held it flat in her lap, turning the pages with a wet thumb, creasing her brow as she read. Tallsman was reading and correcting a thick stack of papers submitted by one of his classes. The papers could neither hold his attention nor conceal his restlessness. His classes studied Cinematic History and Technique. The woman beside him, Corlin McGee, had once been a student of his, not too many years ago, six or seven. She had come a long way since then, but Tallsman wasn't surprised. As a student, Corlin had been a bright girl, and she was surely an equally bright woman now.

"What are you reading?" Tallsman asked her. He placed the papers beside him on the bench and folded his hands in his lap. "Is it more method?"

"Oh, something like that," she said, smiling briefly. She went immediately back to her book, flipping a page.

Tallsman tried again. "Is it a good book?"

"Some of it is, yes." She neither smiled nor glanced up. "Some of it isn't." Licking a thumb, she flipped another page.

Tallsman went back to his papers. The entire stack concerned an old American film he'd shown his lower class the day before, a picture from the thirties titled *Only Angels Have Wings*. It was a good movie, one of Tallsman's personal favorites, and he'd enjoyed seeing it again. But there honestly wasn't much to say about it. The film existed on the screen. All of it was there for a man to see. Tallsman read the top paper. It said: "This is a good film and very enjoyable. I liked it. To say another word would only make me [and it] sound silly." Now that was a good paper, he thought; now that was the truth.

But the one below it began: "The intensity of the scenes between Grant and Mitchell can only be compared in sheer vibrant emotion to the depths of feeling produced by the most unself-conscious of romantic poets."

Tallsman slipped this paper to the bottom of the stack. He turned his eyes away from the next and instead listened to the rain. *Pitter-patter-slap-slap*. He had lived in this country nine years now, but he had never become fully accustomed to the rain. He had originally come from Colorado where, when it rained, it really rained. The sky cracked open and the water came down like a big roaring river. Not here. Here it was strictly *pitter-patter-slap-slap*. A man could walk for hours through a fierce downpour and barely get damp. Tallsman did not even own an umbrella.

"Corlin?" he said.

She glanced up and smiled at him. Briefly.

"Do you own an umbrella?"

"Yes," she said. "I do."

"Just wondered," he said.

The rain came down against the distant wooden roof of the dormitory like the light tiptoeing of a troop of graceful dancers. Gregory Tallsman listened, and the soft rhythm lulled him into a state of near-sleep. He closed his eyes, relaxed his muscles, and floated.

Tallsman had come to New Morning nine years ago, bringing with him a raging enthusiasm for progressive education as it then existed, a sour-faced and pregnant wife named Stephanie, whom he loved, and a future that seemed certain to consist of long bright days of eager teaching. Now, after the rapid passage of those nine years, nothing remained of his original possessions except Stephanie and her sour face. His future had not greatly changed, however. He knew he would continue to teach here at the school, though not with any particular eagerness, at least until the day Joyce Larkin died. Larkin was already in his eighties, but he appeared as healthy and active as any man half his age. When he went, the school would almost certainly go with him, and that would be soon enough for Tallsman to consider other work. Not many schools had a requirement for an instructor in Cinematic History and Technique. Which was mostly why Tallsman stayed at New Morning despite the gradual erosion of his once raging enthusiasm for the school. Or at least this was the reason he gave his wife when she talked about his resigning and their finding a "more suitable place, something better for the children." The reason seemed to satisfy her. As well as anything ever satisfied her. It satisfied him. And that was all that really mattered.

Now the girl, Corlin McGee, she was different. He opened an eye and looked at her. Corlin was a former student and she had gone the full distance and received her certificate. As far as she was concerned, education began and ended within the narrow confines of the school. Not that she knew anything much about education. Not that she was an instructor. Nothing as simple as that. Corlin McGee was an Intensive Therapist. She was Dr. Larkin's strong left arm. To her, the classes were only a necessary evil that had to be tolerated so that the real business of the school could be accomplished with minimal government interference. Tallsman opened his other eye and regarded her closely. Corlin. She was pretty, he thought. She had a certain youthful appeal, he decided. He did not like her. She did not like him. He did not like her because she refused to obey the rules he was forced to endure. He had Stephanie. He had had Stephanie for eleven years. Corlin had Clark Sheridan, who taught physical education. Tallsman hated Clark Sheridan, so why couldn't some sort of trade be arranged? He would hand

Stephanie over to Sheridan (some appropriately dark and stormy night) and take Corlin home with him in return. He had heard that this sort of thing was quite common among the singles in the cities. But not him. He had had to get married, and now look where he was. He smiled, both eyes widely open, and looked straight at the girl. She didn't know he was looking at her. She continued to read. Or did she? Tallsman hastily lowered his eyes and returned to his papers. These long nights of uneventful watching were always an ordeal for him. Why couldn't Larkin simply assign two men to watch with each other? Avoid all these problems. Perhaps he ought to ask. No. He couldn't do that. The old man might get the wrong impression. He decided to try to ignore the girl. He removed the top paper from his stack and read: "What is the truth of existence? How can it most easily be discerned?"

Tallsman looked away. It was twelve-thirty now. That meant he and Corlin had another six hours to spend in each other's exclusive company. He stood and went over and put his ear against the door. He listened for the children but heard nothing. Maybe they had finally gone to sleep. They'd had an hour and a half in which to rid their systems of excess chatter. He turned and coughed. Corlin raised her head and said, "Yes?"

She was going to be polite this time. He realized as he should have realized before that she did not really dislike him. It was only that he did not exist in her private universe, except as a most peripheral figure. Few people did, he thought. There was Sheridan, of course, and the various men who had preceded him. There was Larkin. And the men who wrote the books she was always reading. The children. But who else? Anyone else? Not so far as Tallsman knew. Corlin McGee's universe was a tiny one centered wholly around the grand concept of Intensive Therapy. She and Larkin were the central figures in this universe. But no one else. And certainly not him.

"Did you say something, Greg?"

"Oh," he said. "I'm sorry. I was wondering if I ought to check the beds. I don't hear anything."

"You're worried about them?"

"Of course not. But isn't it better if I check? Then we can both relax for the rest of the night."

"If you want," she said. "But I don't think you'll find what you're looking for. Nothing exciting." Her eyes returned to her book.

Opening the door quietly, Tallsman stepped softly into the darkened room. Fifty-eight children slept here in the north wing. About half were boys and half girls. These were the lower students, aged ten (usually) to thirteen. The older ones, the advanced classes, slept in a parallel wing. Two teachers stood watch over their door as well.

A dim vague light filtered through a half dozen open windows, emanating from the lighted grounds outside. It was bright enough to allow Tallsman to see his own feet as he moved forward. Once he paused and listened but heard nothing other than a great and heavy breathing as if some giant and mythical creature lay fast asleep somewhere in the room.

He moved down the center aisle, stopping occasionally when it wasn't immediately clear whether or not a certain bunk was occupied. He didn't think it very likely that anyone would be missing tonight. It was too wet and cold for any but the most adventuresome to attempt a nocturnal escapade. Besides, all of them knew he was standing watch tonight. He was well known as a prude. Corlin couldn't have cared less if a couple were temporarily absent from the dormitory, but the rules said no, and Tallsman was a man who strongly believed in the rules. In the advanced wing, the rules were different. If any of them wanted to go out, they could, but few ever bothered. Six years ago, Larkin had partitioned two small rooms off the main wing and called them study chambers. It was much cozier there out of the cold and rain. But these children here were only children and the rules said no, so Tallsman studied each bunk carefully, checking for the shape and sound of a breathing body, then moved on to the next.

Ah. He stopped. Here was an empty bed. Obviously so. Not even an attempt at subterfuge, the blankets thrown back and the sheets standing white and clean in the dim light. He made a mental note of the berth number. This was better, he thought. Now let me find the partner.

The second empty bed was two bunks down from the first. Again there had been no attempt at concealment, and Tallsman made a note of number. Then he hurried down the aisle, eager to reach the end. He was forced to pause at the last bunk on the left-hand side when he discovered two girls occupying the lower bed while the upper lay empty. He woke one of the girls and told her to climb up. She did as he asked, and he turned toward the door.

The children followed him down the aisle. Their breathing was individual now, separate and rasping. He knew some of them were surely awake and watching him pass. When they saw him leave, they would move. Perhaps if he only pretended to leave. If he hid and waited and caught them.

But no. Not tonight. Some other night when he wasn't in such a hurry. He went through the door, closed it at his back, and told Corlin: "Two missing. Twenty-nine and thirty-four."

"Always two," she said, absently. She referred to a list. "Twenty-nine is Melissa Brackett," she said. "Which isn't exactly a surprise. Sometimes she amazes me. And thirty-four is"—she flipped a page—"August."

"August?" Tallsman shook his head. "Now that can't be right."

"It is," she said.

"Let me see." He took the list from her and checked the names against the numbers. Well, there still had to be some mistake. Someone was playing a cute little game. August was certainly in that room somewhere. And fast asleep. Tallsman was convinced of that. But where? In someone else's bed, of course. A switch. A cute little joke.

He handed Corlin the list. "Well, it doesn't matter. Whoever's out there, I'll find him."

"No, you won't," she said, standing, turning, getting her coat. "I'll go."

"Let me," he said.

"No." She raised a long narrow object above her head and

shook it at him. The object resembled a black wooden cane wearing a long dark skirt. "My umbrella," she said. "You haven't forgotten?"

"Well, if you want to." He shrugged.

"I want," she said. She turned and headed down the corridor. Her heels tapped loudly, the sound rebounding off the high white walls. Tallsman watched her pass through the outer door and disappear into the darkness beyond.

Then he went back to the bench and sat down and glanced at the spine of the book she had been reading. *Toward a New Psychology of Embryonic Sexuality* by Dalton Godwin. Tallsman let the words run across his tongue several times. They left a bad taste behind. Looking away from the book, he stood and began to shift nervously from foot to foot.

August? Out there? With Melissa Brackett? He had a difficult time restraining himself from open laughter. August was a strange one. Didn't nearly every school, every adolescent or pre-adolescent peer group have its one special strange one? August was the one here at New Morning. Tallsman could clearly recall his own school days. There had been a lot of strange ones back then, and the other children were always able to spot them at once. The strange ones were immediately plucked from among the flock. They were a necessity. They were made victims for the uncontrollable childhood aggressions of the others. Not that things were nearly this stark at New Morning. Not at all. August was a strange one but he was not a victim. If anything, the other children seemed to appreciate him more for his dissimilar behavior. Here was one thing about the school in which Larkin could truly take pride. The children of New Morning did not need victims.

But August was surely a strange one. What was it that made him this way? Tallsman thought, but he could not arrive at a clear answer. August was very small for his age (he was almost thirteen) and he was quiet, shy, and diffident. He had a pair of huge black eyes and a long curling nose. His chin was nearly nonexistent and his skin was pale and white. He was ugly.

Funny-looking. But none of these factors seemed to be enough to provide a full answer.

There was sex. In attitude and appearance August was asexual. This was surely a part of it. But there were several other children of his age who were also late starters. But with them it was clear that they would eventually outgrow this stage. But August? Wouldn't August always remain just as he was now? Tallsman thought so.

August was a strange one.

He had neither parents nor history. None of the children knew this. As far as they were concerned, August was merely another boy. Tallsman was one of the few who knew the truth. He and Larkin had found the boy one summer afternoon four years ago. They had discovered him wandering aimlessly around the school grounds. They stopped and questioned him. He answered (in a strange high lilting voice), claiming he had no name or parents. He couldn't remember his age. Larkin sent Tallsman into town to talk to the authorities. They didn't know. No children reported missing from the local area. Why should there be? And what business was it of theirs? With few exceptions, the local authorities disapproved of Larkin and the school. They would step out of their way to be especially uncooperative. Tallsman went back to the school, and August remained with them. That was how he had gotten his name. August. Because that was when they had found him. August 19. The boy had started at the first level (Larkin had decided he was nine, though he could have been eight or ten) and had managed to blend as well as he ever would. Considering that he was a strange one.

So, where was he now? He was outside, in the wet and cold, huddled underneath the rhododendron (where they always huddled at night) with a girl whose appetite was so enormous for her age that even Larkin joked about it. (But she was supposed to be good, too, and it was more a case of an uncontrollable maternal instinct, rather than anything truly lustful. Melissa was a good girl. Even Tallsman—Tallsman, the prude —even he thought so.)

But August? With her? Now that was absurd.

The door at the end of the corridor opened and Corlin came bustling inside. Pausing in the doorway, she shook herself and dropped the umbrella. Then she hurried forward, forgetting to close the door, forgetting to retrieve the umbrella. She brushed past Tallsman, ignoring his questions, and went to the phone.

She dialed two numbers. And waited.

Tallsman waited too.

She said, "Joyce—this is Corlin."

She said, "Yes, I'm sorry. But I had to wake you. Something has come up. . . . No, I can't explain over the phone. . . . You'll have to come at once. It's August. . . . I'll have to show you. . . . Tallsman. . . . Right, I'll tell him."

She dropped the receiver and said, "Larkin says for us both to wait here."

"Why?" said Tallsman.

"He's coming," she said.

And that was all she would say. After a few minutes, Tallsman stepped down the corridor and shut the door. Then he went back to the bench, sat down, and dropped a stack of papers in his lap. Corlin stood near the phone, shifting from foot to foot. Outside and above the rain went *pitter-patter-slap-slap*.

Tallsman glanced at a paper and read: "The quality of this drama can only be compared with the most intense of—"

He stopped. He folded his hands. He waited.

CHAPTER 3

CORLIN MC GEE:
The Kindly Bush in Bloom

Corlin McGee crouched on the wet ground, balancing precariously on the balls of her feet, and pointed a finger at the overhanging bush. "Look down there. Shine your light. You'll have to. Look."

Dr. Larkin dropped down at her side, and she could almost hear the creaking of his ancient battered bones. He turned the flashlight on the ground beneath the bush and swept the beam from left to right. Corlin turned away. She had seen it once. So why again?

The rain battered at them both (and at Tallsman too—she'd almost forgotten Tallsman, standing alone, neither speaking nor looking) but it wasn't heavy enough to inflict more than minor damage. Larkin squatted on both knees, ignoring the rain and mud, staring at the thing that lay huddled beneath the bush. Corlin wished he would hurry it up. She wanted this whole thing done and over, wanting it to stand as an interesting episode from the past, something to be discussed unemotionally over a cup of tea beside a roaring winter fire, not an immediate and thrusting moment of the present.

She had seen enough. She stood and brushed at her skirt. Tallsman jerked his head questioningly at the bush, and she turned away from him. If he wanted to know, let him look. If Larkin could do it, so could he. If not, let him wait and wonder.

At last Larkin got to his feet and scraped at the mud that lay caked to his trousers. "Do you have a car?"

"No," she said. "Sheridan was going to take me home in the morning."

"I have my car," Tallsman said.

Larkin turned to the other man and nodded his head. He said, "Would you mind getting it for us? I think we ought to take them to my cottage."

"Certainly," Tallsman said. "I'll be happy to do that."

"Corlin, you'll come with me," Larkin said.

"Yes," she said. "I imagine that would be best."

Tallsman nodded, grinning effortlessly, listening to them. Then he turned and hurried away toward the dormitory. Corlin watched his bent, sloping figure scampering through the rain, moving close to the ground as if cowering in fear beneath the inevitable raindrops. What an ignorant and absurd man. Corlin despised almost all the instructors (even Clark, she reminded herself) and Tallsman was even worse than the rest, for Tallsman had his wife with him. And what was he trying to prove with her? Why didn't the whole lot of them—including those two dreadful kids—why didn't they simply pack their bags and move away? Find another part of the world to inflict with their unbearable tediousness?

Oh screw that, she told herself. No reason for that. Tallsman wasn't so terrible, and you can't have a school without a teacher or two, and even if his wife was his wife, he couldn't be held entirely to blame. She was letting this whole incident, this shapeless thing beneath the bush, influence her judgment far too much. And that was wrong.

She crouched down, rocking on her heels, and watched the wide slick rhododendron leaves swaying in the wind. Larkin switched on his flashlight, illuminating the ground beneath the bush, and she shook her head vigorously at him. The light went out. She didn't want to see. She had seen already, so why again?

But the brief flash of light had been enough. She had seen again, and it was worse than it had been before. The two of them were nearly one, a distinct and molded whole, flowing into each other, even the faces, cheek to cheek, and the eyes and lips and noses. Their clothes lay in a neat pile above what was once their heads. He was lying on top of her in a grim caricature of the sexual position. It was like—she searched her mind for a suitable simile—like they had been doing it and then (and when?) a tub of molten steel had suddenly spilled over them both, melting their bodies (but not burning them), drawing them so close together that they would never part.

"I wish he'd hurry," she said to Larkin.

He said, softly, "Now I don't think this is anything to worry about, Corlin." He was breathing heavily, almost gasping between words. "There's nothing we can't handle between us."

"Of course not," she said, still crouching. She fixed an expression on her face that represented womanly competence. It was one of her favorite expressions, and she lifted her hands and allowed Larkin to assist her to her feet. "Are you sure it's him?" she said, when she was standing.

"Who else? Don't say you're surprised."

"Well, not this. He's odd, but why would anyone have expected this?"

"But something like it," he said.

She nodded at that. Something very much like it, yes, for she knew August better than any of them. She had put the boy through Intensive Therapy and had glimpsed more of his true self than he'd ever voluntarily revealed. Even to Larkin.

"What is he?" she said, aloud.

"Now that's a question I can't answer."

"I suppose so," she said.

Hearing the sound of an approaching car, she used the noise as an excuse to drop the conversation. The car came slowly toward them, creeping through the rain, swinging around the bulk of the dormitory, the headlights avoiding the bush, gravel crunching like walnuts beneath the tires. It was a late model station wagon, an automatic, and the cockpit had been inflated to full size.

The car reached them, stopping a few yards from the bush. Tallsman disembarked and said, "Here you go."

"Thank you," said Larkin.

"Do you need any help?"

"No, but thank you. I think you'd better get back to the children. Someone still has to maintain a watch and—do I even have to mention this?—please don't say a word to anyone. You understand this as well as any of us, Greg. You were with me—don't forget—the day we found him. You know he's not like the others. And I believe this will work itself out. I'm sure of it. We'll give it a few days—don't you agree?—and if not, then we'll proceed from that point. Isn't this best?"

"Of course," said Tallsman. He turned immediately and ran through the rain, his arms stiff and steady as posts at his sides.

"You'd better get them. I'll hold the light," Larkin said.

Corlin nodded and bent down. She lowered her eyes until she could barely see more than an occasional brief trace of light. With her fingers she felt beneath the bush. The ground was warm and dry, and then she touched the wet stickiness of molded human flesh. She clutched and pulled and felt the body moving. She pulled harder, digging her heels into the mud. The body came, inch by inch, and at last she heard the rain pattering noisily against the bare flesh. Releasing her hold, she turned away, opened her eyes, and sucked at the moist clean fresh air.

"Splendid," said Larkin. "Now for the end."

He helped her with the rest of it, moving the body the few remaining yards to the car, forcing it through the narrow side door, placing it evenly on the floor of the large storage area behind the rear seat. When that was done, they got into the car together, sitting in the front seat. Corlin took the wheel and saw that Tallsman had already adjusted the directional coordinates to Larkin's cottage. She put the car in gear, felt its answering thrust of power and motion, then turned to the side window.

Beside her, Larkin was breathing heavily in his ancient gasping way, but she chose to ignore his presence, concentrating instead upon the dark shadows of the passing night. The car bumped easily along the rocky ground beside the gently flowing creek. Larkin's cottage was only a few hundred yards from the dormitory, and the trip was not long. The car soon halted obediently, and the two of them got out and went to the back. They did not speak, and this was fine with Corlin. Together they carried the body into the cottage, went to a back bedroom, placed it on the bed, and covered it with a blanket so that only the molded face protruded. And that was what it was too. One face for two people. A pair of bright shining eyes, neither brown nor blue and certainly not black—a mouth and dry lips —a nose—ears—features that awkwardly combined the distinctive components of both Melissa and August, molding them into a true oneness that was neither he nor she, boy nor girl, that was someone else entirely, a new person in the world. But who? thought Corlin. And what?

They went into the living room.

Corlin turned and faced Larkin. Her hands dropped to her sides, and she felt her lips and chin trembling as she sought to form an expression of firm defiance on her face. She wanted to appear strong and stoic and unmoved, but it couldn't be done. She couldn't do it. Not alone. She needed help.

Larkin must have seen her ambivalence. Turning his back, he disappeared quickly into the kitchen, leaving her alone in the room. She stood and listened to him moving in the back and thought how he had lived within these same walls for nearly thirty years, ever since the day the school had opened. At the peak of his fame, when the school was booming with as many as three hundred pupils and his books were selling thousands upon thousands of copies, he was earning more than enough money to allow him to move into town and live in real style, but he had always preferred the quiet, secluded life. This place suited him well, the four small rooms, the cloistered atmosphere, the rows of books and tapes, the pale and white walls and ceiling. There wasn't an unnecessary object in the entire house. She knew. Once she had tried to find one. Everything was ultimately functional.

She called out: "I'm going now, Joyce."

"Oh, Corlin," he called back. "Oh, fine. And stop by tomorrow if you get the chance."

"I'll do that," she said, turning, leaving, stepping into the rain. She walked slowly to the car and got inside, automated it, and moved again along the creek. She was thinking about how she had once worshiped that man, back when she was his student, overwhelmed by his life and theories, unable to imagine an existence not centered around Joyce Larkin and Intensive Therapy and New Morning school. Well, she'd surely gotten the life she had desired. She knew more about the uses and methods of Intensive Therapy than anyone alive, except Larkin himself, and she had written articles and one book and answered endless questions, and during the past few years while Larkin's own interest had seemed to fade, it had been she more than anyone who had kept the school alive and functioning. But she couldn't help remembering her school days, when a glance from Larkin, a brief and passing smile, was enough to leave her deliriously happy for weeks at a time. She had even slept with Rogirsen twice when she was seventeen (and suffering the depths of puppy love) because she couldn't sleep with Larkin himself and Rogirsen was the man closest to Larkin and he had had to suffice.

She had only done it twice. That had been enough.

But she almost wanted him now. Rogirsen, poor mad Rogirsen (it had taken her twice to realize that), yes, she almost wanted him now. The incident, the episode, the event, the thing under the bush. It had affected her in a way she would not have predicted. Where had all her cold and scientific training gone when faced with a situation that was truly impossible? It had disappeared, gone, fled, and how was she going to get it back? It wasn't what had happened so much as it was the way in which it had happened. Why had it occurred when they were screwing? Why not when they were cutting wood, or mowing the lawn, or talking, or watching one of Tallsman's moldy movies? Why not then?

The sight of the two of them locked together had been like seeing a sudden and broken and twisted fantasy image of herself and some anonymous man. It hadn't touched Larkin that way, of course. Sex was not an actuality for him. But for her, at twenty-three, a woman, for her it was exactly like witnessing the enactment of her deepest fantasy wishes on a lighted stage beneath a rhododendron bush. Clutching. Drawing closer. Bellies rubbing, hands grasping, scratching, down, thrusting, closer and closer. Hold me. Scratching. Smothering. Oh! Closer! How much closer? No more closer! *Together. One. Free! Oh free!*

Yes and no wonder. Wasn't that what she was always striving for? Wasn't that what she was really seeking in the endless repetition of the act? To be drawn so close to the man above (or below or behind) that she ceased to exist as an individual entity, that she became instead only an extension of him, drawn ever closer, deeper, until suddenly—*ping*—oblivion. She wasn't there any more. Corlin McGee? Who? There must be some mistake. There is no such thing as a Corlin McGee. I'm quite certain of that. She's only a part of that other one. That man. Oh, what is his name? Rogirsen, I think, or Sheridan or whomever.

Or Tallsman, perhaps. Right now, the way she felt, even him.

And why not? This wasn't the first time she had imagined sex with Tallsman, and so what if he was married? Honestly. Customs and mores come and go, constantly changing. What is correct and proper for one era may appear ridiculous (or perverse) in another. Marriage was considered a sacred institution at this particular moment in history, and why was that? Only because of its comparative rarity, because people married late in life, in their thirties and forties and fifties, after years of careful exploration, because mistakes were rare, because nobody would think of marrying for sex alone. Because the present establishment, the government, was able to combine liberal morality with conservative politics and make it work. Because Tallsman's marriage was surely a mistake. Because his wife was awful. So why couldn't he? And she? So why couldn't she?

When the car stopped at the dormitory, she bounded up the steps and raced down the corridor, going straight for Tallsman, and he watched her coming, and she studied his eyes, searching for the reaction she sought, and found it (perhaps) and fell into his arms, fell flat against him, his hands at his sides, clutching.

"Oh," she said. "Did you see it, Greg? Wasn't it—? Oh, Greg, can't you tell me?"

"Corlin," he said, but not moving.

She looked at his face, his trembling lips, and said, "Help me, can't you see, help me, please."

And he put his arms around her. He held her in his arms.

But it wasn't any use. She felt the heaviness of his bulging waistline, the chill of his flesh, the flatness of his expression. His hands grew weak and tired and loose. Aimlessly, he stroked the flesh of her back.

She pulled away, turned her back. His hands touched her shoulders.

He said, "I'm sorry. I didn't look. Remember? I never saw it."

"That's right," she said. "That's all right, Greg."

They sat down together on the bench. She stared at the wooden door, beyond which slept the children, and he stared at her and the night passed away.

Pitter-patter, said the rain. *Pitter-patter-slap-slap.* The sun rose. Before that, the rain stopped.

CHAPTER 4

MICHAEL ROGIRSEN:
The Eagle Took His Eye

Having seen both of them just this morning walking together through the faint misty light of early dawn with their heads so close and nearly touching and conversing in whispers so soft that it was impossible for him to overhear, even allowing for his secret (to them) and famous (to him) talent of being able to hear sounds not audible to any normal man. This was, of course, because of the red Indian blood which coursed constantly through his veins but which Larkin had deliberately kept from him until the day he'd found the secret himself, concealed behind the old man's desk, and learned the full truth of his once hidden existence, fully realizing for the first time in his life that Larkin was a liar, a man never to be trusted, one of them, a man whose sole purpose in life was preventing him from fulfilling the totality of his fated destiny.

He peered through the front window of the cottage, then slipped around to the back and peeked through another window. (Larkin, being as casual as possible, never covered his windows —or perhaps not—Rogirsen was beginning to glimpse the truth in this—perhaps Larkin was acting deliberately in order to ease his suspicions and then one day lure him unaware into the cottage and there—with the assistance of the woman—to mutilate, humiliate, torture, and destroy.) This was something well worth considering, and Rogirsen proceeded with the utmost of caution.

He turned and went around to the front of the cottage where

it faced the near-by creek. The rain had stopped several hours before, but the dirt at his feet was wet and soft, and his footprints followed him from front to back, then from back to front. The creek rolled noisily past, his keen Indian ears picking up the bubbling swish of passing fish, and his prints would serve as a reminder to both of them that he was not unaware of their plotting, that he was very strong and fully dedicated and willing to fight for his life. His feet cut deeply into the wet molding earth, and his tracks followed him to the front door.

Rogirsen tried the knob. The door was not locked. He was not surprised; the door was never locked. For a long moment, he stood with his hand resting easily on the knob. Michael Rogirsen was a sly man. Cunning. He glanced casually over one shoulder and immediately noted the suspicious character of the land, its utter desolation, and the sudden, almost questioning silence of the creek. He looked above, studying the gray sky for signs of life. A spying aircraft; a balloon; a helicopter. They had used all these tactics against him in the past and he was ever vigilant to prevent a repetition of their previous success. He had a motto: *Once bitten—twice shy.* You could fool him once, but not twice.

For example, there was the incident with the bird. That was one Rogirsen recalled with a clarity that was nothing short of frightening. Larkin had built an artificial bird in his laboratory at the school. The bird, despite its mechanical origins, possessed all the appearances of natural life, from blood to belly, from feathers to beak. Larkin had released the bird to the sky. Sent it spying. On him. On Rogirsen. It had taken him three days and three nights to trap the creature. When he had, chuckling with delight, laughing with glee, he had made himself a meal of the thing, a surprisingly tasty dish; but then, in a momentary flash of insight, the truth had dawned on him. Larkin had known. He had known in advance exactly what he would do. And the bird was inside him. Spying. Relaying the most private of knowledge to its master. He had vomited again and again, cleansing his body of every last trace of the tainted bird, and what a memory, so pure and clear, like a minute ago, the last of it swirling madly down toward the bowels of the island. He'd won that battle but the war was far from done.

Enough of that. Rogirsen entered the cottage. He was careful in closing the door; he was careful in crossing the room. Some trace of his entrance could not be avoided, for Larkin kept strands of taut animal hair stretched across certain portions of the room, strands so fine as to be nearly invisible to the naked eye, and he knew he could not reach his destination without disturbing one or two. Still, he was careful. And still, it was worth the danger.

If it hadn't been for last night, none of this would have been necessary. But what had happened and some sort of response was now unavoidable. It was her. The woman. All white woman and damn her, come creeping into his sleeping place and her wanting and demanding him while knowing all along the poison they fed him made it impossible for him to escape the ultimate humiliation. And it had gone as it had always gone with the woman, and she'd laughed and cried, had her fun, toyed with him like some smothering jungle snake all wrapped around and moaning like a snake, spitting, clawing, weeping like a snake.

Then later, done with him, she'd gone to Larkin and told him everything. This was the part Rogirsen could never forgive. He'd heard their every word (his red Indian blood coursing), even through the noise of the creek, the pattering of the rain, and together they'd had their laugh, then made their plans, whispering this last so that he could not hear. But he could guess, which was why he was here; it wasn't hard to guess.

The bed would fix everything. Once he reached the bed.

He moved quickly now. He went straight for the back bedroom, where once upon a long time ago he had lived and slept and where the process had begun, the pushing him back to places he did not want to go. Back and back. Stop—no!—back. He remembered that too.

The door was open. He went into the bedroom.

Wait.

What? What was it? He stood and looked and this was something new. A . . . thing. That was what it was. All man and woman and done into one and neither and lying on the bed, playing at sleep and—but, no, wait, the eyes were opening.

Looking at him.

The eyes were grinning. Then the lips, the mouth.

"Hello," it said.

Get away.

"Rogirsen," it said. "August."

Rogirsen turned away. August? No, it couldn't be August, because August was a friend. This was merely a trick. Larkin's way of driving them apart. Larkin didn't want him to have friends, so he had made this thing in his laboratory (like the bird—exactly like that) and—

"Rogirsen. Me."

No. Rogirsen put his hands over his ears, his keen sharp Indian red ears. He refused to listen. But the thing stood and came forward and touched him.

"Rogirsen. Look at me. Michael."

He would not look. Running. Out through the living room and out through the door, snapping a thousand strands of taut animal hair, snapping them like a spider's web, running, out across the grounds, toward the gleaming gash of the rushing creek.

The fish were crying. Come to us and we will wash you clean. Oh, Rogirsen. Diving into the water, he clawed at the mud. He screamed, wept, begged.

Oh, Rogirsen. And above in the sky a million eyes flickered, blue eyes, blinked, brown eyes, blotting out the sun, red eyes, black, opened, all eyes, then stared at him.

Oh, Rogirsen.

The eyes.

CHAPTER 5

GREGORY TALLSMAN:
Ash and Water

Tallsman stood at the front of the classroom and rubbed his eyes. Other days and other times. He couldn't help remembering when he'd weave homeward after a long night of wakeful watching and slip between warm sheets after a breakfast of bacon and eggs and orange juice and toast. None of this was extraordinary, he knew, but it was the ordinary things in life, the most conventional and most enjoyable that Tallsman liked best. Right now he would happily settle for just that. He'd even forego the breakfast of eggs and bacon and juice and toast if, in return, he was allowed the comforting warmth of the sheets. He was exhausted, half dead on his feet. And the class kept staring at him, expectantly waiting.

He shook his head, sweeping his mind, and tried to return their stares. The vacant seats easily outnumbered the occupied ones today, mostly because of the big red sun, which had suddenly cracked the dull gray sky about an hour ago, and Tallsman forced himself to make a quick count and entered the two-digit number (but barely) on the proper line of the official government form. He taught only two classes a day, both two hours in length, the first beginning at ten, the second at noon. It was ten o'clock and this was his most enjoyable class, the advanced seniors. The movies he screened here were usually better, more able to withstand frequent viewings, and the students themselves were more apt to say something new and interesting. In the old days, when he was a younger and more idealistic man, he had often said that he loved teaching because it provided him an opportunity to continue learning throughout his life. You can learn more from a child than you can ever teach him, Tallsman used to say back then. He hadn't said anything like that in many years, but he still believed it. Sometimes he still believed it. Like now. He believed it now.

He clapped his hands once, and the class fell silent. He said, "Did anybody happen to bring anything with them today? Anything good, I mean."

Four hands went into the air, three with adolescent certainty and the fourth more tentatively.

"Good, good," said Tallsman. "That means I won't have to talk. That means we can go ahead and look at some of our own work. Tomorrow I'll have some good things to show, so if you see anybody who's not here today be sure and tell them to come."

Then he turned away and went to the back of the room and took a seat. He had decided to pass the two hours quickly by letting the students show their own films. With the lights extinguished, he could relax and besides, very often the films were well worth watching. Tallsman had seen a great many talented people pass through his classes over the years. Some had even progressed all the way into the professional world of film-making and Mentatape, and this had made him very proud.

While his mind drifted, the students scurried about and arranged the room for the screening. The lights were switched off, the shades were drawn, and the projector and screen were readied. Without warning, the first film began. Tallsman watched the initial footage. The opening was the usual for an outdoor film, a shot of the rolling creek with Larkin's cottage looming whitely in the background. Two people could be seen distantly moving beside the cottage. The camera forded the creek and bumped ahead in order to observe the people. Tallsman laid his head in his hands and closed his eyes. The film continued. Tallsman was fairly certain he had seen this one before, and if not, he doubted he was missing much. Not necessarily because of the opening shot. Larkin's cottage was the only suitable location on the school grounds, except for the old caretaker's cottage, and that was where Rogirsen lived, and the students were afraid of Rogirsen. Except for August. August and Rogirsen were good friends, frequent companions.

Which put Tallsman back in a place he did not care to visit. With August. And Corlin. In the dormitory, then outside and watching as two separate and individual human beings became a single entity and while Larkin mumbled and stumbled and acted old and dying. And then it was morning and back with Stephanie, and she was dashing at him like a hungry bear as he pulled himself into the house, and she snapped at him, munched at him, rending his flesh and demanding: *what was this?* and *why was that?* and *who was she?* and *why won't you answer me?*

But he was answering her. Every trivial Stephanie question was getting its proper reply.

"I can tell something went wrong out there last night and I'm not even going to ask you what. I just can't see it. Tell me why. Why do we have to stay here when both of us hate it?"

"You know why. There's no place else to go."

"Government school. I still don't see that. You're a good teacher, aren't you? You believe in their system. You do, don't you? And so if—"

"Because they don't have classes in—"

"But that shouldn't matter. You're loyal, aren't you? That's what ought to matter, and I bet I know what it is. Guilt is what it is. Just that. If we'd never come here, if we'd only known in advance how it was, we could do it now."

"No, that's—"

"Stop it! Can't you see that I can't stand any more of this?"

She went on. The children had refused to sleep. The rain frightened them and disgusted her. Why do we have to live here? Why can't we go and—?

He had been sorely tempted. Tallsman grinned at his hands. He could have told her during one of those rare moments when she was forced to pause for air. So you think something went wrong last night. You say you can see by the way I'm acting.

Well, maybe you're right this time. Dear. You see, it was this way. August and Melissa went outside to screw beneath the rhodedendron, and I disapprove of that sort of thing because you've made it certain that I can't very well approve, and I went in and found their beds empty, so Corlin went outside to bring them back and she found them, yes, they were under the bush, but they were all molded together. I think that's the best way of putting it. I got a good look but I wouldn't let anyone know. Molded together, each absorbed by the other, as though a tub of molten steel had spilled over them at the peak of their activities. Do you see it now? Is it clear in your mind? Or do you have a sheet of blank white paper around? Maybe a drawing from life would help in making the scene clear in your fat and bloated brain. Dear.

But he hadn't said that, hadn't said a word, maneuvering her so that he could break for the bedroom and grab a quick nap before he had to return to school for his ten o'clock class. Not that she was about to allow him that. She hadn't been able to sleep last night. Not with that driving slashing pounding rain beating down on the roof as though the Great Flood had come again.

Somebody was shaking him. "Hey, Tallsman, wake up—there's something outside."

He opened his eyes, squinting. The lights were on and the students stood beside the windows facing the creek. Stifling his embarrassment at being caught napping, he pushed between two of them and looked outside.

"Get back to your chairs. You've seen this. Now go."

"Look at him out there. The old goof."

"All of you stay here," Tallsman said.

He went into the corridor and headed toward the outer doors, knowing it was strictly up to him to settle this. For reasons he had never fully understood, Rogirsen trusted him. Only two other people—Larkin and Corlin—were able to handle him when he was in the midst of one of his fits, and they did it with fear rather than trust. And for good reasons too. Larkin was the one who had made Rogirsen what he was—Intensive Therapy's one and glaring failure—while Corlin, as a girl, had ensured that he would never change.

Tallsman ran across the grass. In the distance, Rogirsen danced, stumbling in the creek, water splashing as he pounded it with his fists as though the creek were a living creature able to feel pain. At least he wasn't likely to drown. Not unless he tripped and fell and hit his head. Even in the middle, the creek was less than three feet deep.

Tallsman drew closer. He had stopped running, but now he began again, because there was another person in the water with Rogirsen, trying to subdue him. Tallsman hurried. He had recognized the other man. It was Sheridan. The physical education instructor and Corlin's good friend. Tallsman turned as he ran and shook his fist at the school. The windows were dotted with the faces of peering students. He turned back to the creek. The faces stayed.

By the time he reached the water, Sheridan had Rogirsen on the edge of the bank. He was squatting over him, his knees holding the other man's arms pinned to the ground.

"Let him up," Tallsman said.

Sheridan shook his head, panting. His clothes were soaked.

"I can handle him," Tallsman said.

Sheridan turned around. A wide streak of blood ran down his forehead, past his eyes, crossing his lips and jaw.

"Come on," Tallsman said. "This isn't helping."

Sheridan moved away and got to his feet. He set himself for trouble but Rogirsen remained flat on his back. Sheridan wiped at the blood on his face. Rogirsen grinned widely at the sky.

Tallsman crouched down. The creek streamed past, only inches away, and Rogirsen's worn dirty clothes were drenched with water. Tallsman said, "You'd better go home, Michael. You're wet."

"Catch cold?"

"You might. Here—would you like me to help you."

"Yes," Rogirsen said.

Tallsman helped the other man to his feet. Rogirsen shook

himself like an animal and rubbed at his clothing. He looked at Sheridan, then past him, through him, as though he weren't really there. "Better go home," he said.

"I think that's a good idea, Michael. You're very wet."

"A good day. Day for swimming."

"Yes."

"You're wondering. Thinking I'm crazy again."

"No. Whatever you do, it's all right with me. You're a free man, Michael. I don't mind."

"Larkin puts a thing in his house. Thing tries to kill me. Some kind of thing."

Tallsman said, "Oh."

"You're thinking I'm lying again." Rogirsen swiveled his head and pointed it across the creek at the cottage. "Thing is still there. Go and look. Might not try and kill you."

"It can't hurt you if you're home, Michael."

Rogirsen nodded and grinned. Three of his front teeth were missing. "Too quick," he said, then walked off, dripping water. As he moved, his narrow hips jerked and swayed. He rubbed at his head, and twice he turned and waved at Tallsman.

Tallsman waved back.

Sheridan dabbed his sleeve at his forehead. He said, "Fought like a tiger. Knocked me down and banged my head against a rock."

"Better go see the nurse."

"I'll live. It's only a cut, but why they let a nut like him run around loose I'll never understand. You tell me. And these kids. It's a miracle he hasn't killed one yet."

"He's harmless."

"So far." Sheridan lost interest in his forehead but the blood kept flowing. He turned away.

Tallsman said, "He's harmless." He was waiting for Sheridan to leave. He wanted to go to the cottage and see the thing that was waiting there. But he wanted to go alone.

Sheridan said, "What happened with you and Corlin last night?" His back still faced Tallsman. Was he ashamed of the blood?

"Nothing," Tallsman said.

"She came home this morning like something had happened. I just wondered."

"Nothing happened."

"Well, keep your secrets if you want them. I've got to get back to my kids. I'll see you later, Tallsman."

"Right," said Tallsman. He sat down on the ground and watched the tumbling creek rolling past. He waited until he was certain Sheridan had gone, then waded through the water, heading for the cottage.

Why had they brought the body to the cottage anyway? Hadn't anyone had sense enough to remember that Rogirsen would surely come poking around the next day? Tallsman hadn't thought of it, but Larkin should have known.

The front door was open. He pushed and stepped inside, stopping in the middle of the living room and listening. Then he laughed at himself. What had he expected to hear? The shuffling step of a caged monster?

He stepped quickly and bravely down the hall to the rear bedroom, but when he got there all he found was an empty bed and a wrinkled orange sheet.

He went into the other bedroom and glanced at the kitchen and went outside and circled the cottage. Then he put his hands to his lips and cried: "August! Melissa! Where are you?"

Then he turned and hurried away, heading toward the school.

CHAPTER 6

JOYCE LARKIN:
Reporting the Buried Life

Sitting behind his bare slick desk, rocking and rolling in a padded chair, his hands firmly clasped across his chest, Joyce Larkin thought contented thoughts of death and dying. These were the subjects which at eighty-two concerned him more concretely than all the other myriad subjects of heaven and earth rolled into one. Death was a constant presence. Right now, as he sat rocking, it rocked with him, pulsing beneath his folded hands. Larkin suffered from cancer of the lungs; he was dying from cancer of the stomach. The combined activities of the disease consumed a bit of him each passing hour until, with a sigh, he momentarily left his life and school and went to the city and the machines toyed with him and when he came home he brought another six months of life with him and added those days onto the eighty-odd years he had previously been granted.

The cancer in his lungs was less significant, on the whole, than the older, more advanced growth in his stomach, but lately he'd spent many more hours contemplating the newer growth and had tended to ignore the older one. The cancer in his stomach had been discovered ten years ago while the growth in his lungs had been there less than six months, had been arrested only once by the pulsating government machines. It was about time to go again, he knew. He could feel it moving in there, both places, tentatively groping forward, wondering *Have I got him now? Has he finally given it up? Will I get my fill of him this time?*

No, he wanted to tell it, tell both of them, old malignant stomach and new growling lungs, *you have not got him this time. Nor will you ever.*

But why not? Why not go ahead and die? There was, after all, no pressing reason why he ought to continue to live. Nothing, in fact, except for the barren pleasure of continued conscious awareness. A few more breaths of air. A couple of flowers to be smelled. What else? Little else.

They had him right where they wanted him, imprisoned in a cage without bars, and he could free himself only by dying. They had told him that ten years ago. We'll be happy to save you, Larkin, but there are a few minor things we'll expect you not to do in return. That's right. We're not asking you to do anything for us. Only asking you not to do a few minor things. Don't push ahead. Keep your school, but don't improve it. Don't train a successor. When you die, we'd prefer to see New Morning go with you. It is a bit of an anachronism, you know, better dead and buried in this modern age. Under these conditions, however, we'll gladly tolerate its continued existence and yours as well. If you stop doing nothing, then we'll have to start doing nothing, and within a few months you'll be dead and buried and, presumably, your school with you. So what do you say, Larkin? Is it a bargain? We can start treatment this very moment, if you so desire. No point to waiting, is there?

No point. And he had so desired. That was the substance of the bargain he had accepted and the bargain he had kept. If in order to stave off death he had to do nothing, then he would do nothing. And he had. Not for ten years, and the results were surprisingly obvious. The school was dying. The student population had declined to half its peak figure. Contributions had slowly but surely dwindled away. New classes, experimental methods and techniques, teacher/pupil involvement, all of these were things of the past. His instructors were no longer the best in the world. The few new ones who drifted in came in search of peace and tranquility. They wanted security and this was what they found. New Morning was a safe place, unexciting but pleasant and secure.

Twenty years ago, it had been different. Joyce Larkin had taken pride in the fact that he had managed to cram two hundred years of living into the first six decades of his life. He had come into the world in the good year of 1922, never knowing his father but unable to avoid the glorious domination of his mother. Once the two of them, mother and son, had gotten together in an attempt to discover once and for all the true identity of Joyce's father. Martha Larkin could not have cared less. Joyce was her son; why should she share him with some strange man whom she hardly knew? But Joyce had insisted that he must know and they went over a list of names, eventually trimming the possibilities to three. Joyce went looking, found two of the men, both actors, and promptly crossed them off his list. He did not like them. He could discover nothing of himself in their pale dull features. The third man could not be found. In 1932 he had disappeared into the interior of China, intent upon joining the Communist movement there, and had never been seen again. Joyce settled on this man as his father. Nobody could ever prove otherwise.

But he did not really need a father, living or dead. He should have known this. His mother was more than enough parent for any man or boy. Martha Larkin had never been a really big star, probably because unlike most of her Hollywood contemporaries she was an excellent dramatic actress, having spent ten years on the legitimate New York stage before coming to California in search of wealth and fame and a good home and (most importantly) a clean and suitable environment in which to raise her son. She was twice nominated for the Academy Award in supporting character roles, but never won. It didn't bother her particularly. Unlike most of her contemporaries, she was a truly searching woman, whose intellectual pretensions were considerably more than that. She enjoyed music, art, literature (particularly the *avant-garde,* though she was well able to separate the true experimenters from the flock of fakers who surrounded them), dabbled in radical politics, and liked good clothes. Men she found universally boring.

As a boy, Joyce enjoyed an excellent education. Through

various means, always legal but seldom fair, his mother gained entrance for him to a string of prestigious Eastern schools and academies, culminating in a degree from Princeton (Harvard proving too much even for Martha Larkin) in 1944. Joyce skipped the war—it didn't interest him—and got a job, and within five years his column, *Hollywood Eavesdroppings,* was syndicated in nearly two hundred newspapers worldwide. It was a better-than-average column too. Most of his information was accurate and there was considerable space devoted to the real product of Hollywood (movies) rather than the more artificial glamor of the town (stars). Then television came along and his column lost much of its popularity (Joyce refused to look at television—it wasn't his medium) and his mother died in 1950 at the age of sixty-three, leaving her estate in the hands of her last husband, a man three years younger than Joyce.

Not having much else to do except mourn and grieve, Joyce kept writing his column for several years. In 1963 he finally dropped it completely, though by this time fewer than twenty papers were continuing to run it. Then he went back to school and got himself another degree. He liked it, so he got another one, and within a few years he was correctly known as Dr. Joyce Larkin, and he went up to Yale and started teaching undergraduates the facts and theories of psychology. He hated the work. So he quit after a year, looked up a lot of old friends, and with their money formed his own school. He called it New Morning and tucked it away in a distant corner of the country where nobody could see it unless they went especially looking for it. He got the best teachers and put them to work. He developed some methods and wrote a book about them. But it still did not seem as if it were quite enough, so he developed Intensive Therapy and made it the essential part of his educational curriculum. He wrote another book and got denounced.

Intensive Therapy was either a fascinating combination or a wholesale theft (depending on whom you read) from the entire history of psychology and psychoanalysis, including several theorists normally accepted as crackpots. Basically, Larkin took the average ten-year-old (the perfect age, he felt) and forced the child to relive his life, then his birth, then beyond, and finally beyond even that until the child was simultaneously living and reliving all of his lives (and there were a great many, Larkin discovered). When it was over and done, the therapy complete, the child should have been a well and whole human being. Of course, it never happened this way, but it worked well enough to satisfy Larkin. He became a famous man again. The children of the rich and powerful poured through the gates of his school. He kept them for a maximum of nine years, then turned them loose on the world. For the most part, they worked out very well.

Until, that is, the day he caught cancer of the stomach and chose to sell himself to a new and less bold government at the price of his own life. After that, it was over and done, the glory was gone, but he kept on living and kept on wondering why.

And then there was last night. Last night might well have been the beginning of the end. If so, Larkin welcomed it. He was ready; he was not afraid.

He said, "Come in." He had ignored the knocking the first time it had come, but the second series of raps had sounded quite insistent. "The door's open."

A small man with slick black hair, brown skin, and a sloping face that tapered into a weak chin entered the room. The man wore a tight-fitting brown uniform with two silver bars on each shoulder. He carried a gun at his waist, and his name was Antonio Milinqua. He was area supervisor for the island and he often visited Larkin.

"Hello, Antonio," said Larkin.

"I'm not interrupting you?"

"No. Oh no. I was merely thinking. I knew it was you at the door. The children never knock. They march right in."

"Which is why I am glad that my children do not attend your school. I would not appreciate their bad manners."

"You don't have any children."

Milinqua sat down in a stiff-backed wooden chair across from Larkin's desk. He looked comfortable and he crossed his short thin legs at the ankles. He said, "That's true."

"Then what can I do for you?" Larkin said. "You didn't come all the way out here for a simple chat."

"No, I didn't. I'm afraid this is an official matter, Joyce. But a simple thing. Of no great significance. It's merely an excuse, you might say, for a chat."

"That's fine," said Larkin, smiling. He crossed his hands over his stomach, then jerked them suddenly away. He dropped them flat on his desk and hoped Milinqua had failed to notice the abruptness of his action. He could wait no longer. He would have to seek immediate treatment in the city. He had felt that thing in there, that cancer in his stomach, had felt it reaching out and grasping hungrily at the warm tingling flesh of his hands.

"I need a listing of your students," Milinqua said. "Their names, parents' names, addresses."

"Why?" Larkin asked.

"An order."

"But why come to me?"

Milinqua was not telling the truth, which intrigued Larkin. As far as the island was concerned, he was supreme lord and master. He took orders from no one locally. Nor was his task a minor one. There were several government installations on the island, including a large secret research station on the southeastern tip.

"You don't have such a list?"

"Oh, I have one. But so does your machine. Why not ask it?" Larkin knew Milinqua was merely playing a game with him. He also realized that the man was doing it for his benefit.

"I'm asking you. Now, Joyce, please." He reached across the desk and his smile enlarged. "I must have this list."

Before Larkin could reply, the door opened, interrupting him. A boy of twelve or thirteen bounded into the room as quick as a ball. The boy was fat, tall, and redheaded, with freckles as big and thick as measles dotting his face and arms. The boy said, "Hi, Larkin. Who's this?"

Larkin introduced the boy, whose name was Steven, to Antonio Milinqua. Milinqua said, "Hi, Steve."

The boy said, "Hi, Tony," and came toward Larkin. He said, "I've got to use your typewriter for a minute, Larkin."

"Why?" said Larkin.

"Because I have to send a letter to my mother. What do you think? You think I'm writing a book of poems?" The boy stopped, put his feet together, and glared at Larkin, fists against hips, elbows jutting like sharp spears. "Nobody will let me use their vocorders. I broke mine and they think I'll break theirs."

"Will you?" Larkin asked. Milinqua was twitching impatiently. Larkin ignored him. He had never seen Milinqua twitch before, and he was enjoying the sight. Steven had come at the exact proper time.

"It was an accident," the boy said. "So what?"

"Will you break mine?"

"You don't have one."

"I mean my typewriter."

"Of course I won't break it. Why should I?"

"All right," Larkin said, slowly. "I'll trust you." He vacated his chair and allowed the boy to take possession. He went over and sat down beside Milinqua. The stiff-backed chair was like steel against his frail bones. He muttered with discomfort. The boy jerked the cover off the typewriter, blew a cloud of dust, inserted a sheet of blank paper, and began to peck away at the keyboard.

"The list," said Milinqua.

"Oh," said Larkin. "One moment." Happily accepting the opportunity to move, he stood and went into an adjoining room that had once been used by his secretary when he'd had a secretary. He opened a filing cabinet and removed a folder. He thumbed through the contents of the folder and then closed it and carried it back to his office. Milinqua plucked the folder from his fingers and opened it in his lap.

Larkin remained on his feet. The boy pecked away at the typewriter. He asked Larkin how to spell *resplendent* and Larkin told him.

Milinqua said, "This list isn't complete. A boy is missing."

"No," Larkin said. "That's it."

"This list is the same as the one I have."

"But doesn't that—?"

"How do you spell *ramifications?*"

Larkin told him.

"There's a name missing on both lists. A boy. We have a record. Surely you recall the incident. The boy appeared here several years ago, mysteriously. He was taken in. We have a full record of the incident. One of your teachers came to us."

"That's right," Larkin said.

"Where is he?"

"In his classroom."

"The boy? August?"

"No. The teacher. Tallsman."

"I want the boy."

"I can't tell you," Larkin said.

"But—" said Milinqua. He was interrupted by the office door opening. A head popped through and was gone again before anyone could put a name to it.

Larkin said, "I'm sorry, Antonio."

Milinqua said, "I must have this boy. I hate to say this. You and I have always been friendly, if never friends. But this is of the utmost importance to us. If you do not let me have this boy, then I must tell you. I will make a full and complete report regarding this conversation. If I file this report—"

"How do you spell *necessities?*"

"Shut up," Milinqua said.

Larkin spelled the word for the boy.

Then Milinqua continued: "If I report this, I will be forced to make a recommendation. Your treatments for cancer will be discontinued. I think you know the result. You will die. Now—think. Is it worth it? This one boy."

"The boy isn't here. He's not in the school."

"I'm sorry," Milinqua said. "You have until noon tomorrow. I owe you that much. In the meantime, my men are searching your buildings. If they happen to find the boy, I will forget this conversation. My report will be favorable."

"The boy isn't in the school," Larkin said.

"I am sorry," Milinqua said again. He reached into his tunic and removed a folded paper. He handed the paper to Larkin and said, "Official Emergency Situation. This authorizes my search." He went for the door.

He was gone.

Larkin sat down in the chair Milinqua had vacated. He clasped his hands together around the paper. He put his hands in his lap.

The door opened. Tallsman entered, glancing at the boy, then at Larkin. He said, "I have to see you alone, Doctor. It's very important."

"All right," Larkin said.

CHAPTER 7

JOYCE LARKIN:
The Sunset Was Brief Like
a Dying Man's Breath

They ignored the buildings, the school and dormitory, the two small cottages, his and Rogirsen's, knowing that Milinqua would search them competently and thoroughly but checking back after an hour to ensure that nothing had been found. Nothing had been found, and so they swept wide in their search and began to peck at the edge of the woods, then to infringe upon it, then to search it as thoroughly as possible. There were few trails in the woods. On the whole it was as deep and dark and impenetrable as a Louisiana swamp. Even the children seldom ventured far into the woods. Their first few weeks, sometimes they did since it was something new and strange. Those first few weeks it was the enchantment and nearness of real trees and flowers and vines and ferns. But that did not last, a week, two weeks, never more, not for those who were well-adjusted. Anything that could be done within the woods could as easily be done without, and there were children outside the woods who laughed and talked and played, and there was nothing inside the woods except real trees and flowers and vines and ferns. And silence. Trees and flowers and vines and ferns do not talk. Or laugh. The children were afraid of the silence.

So there were only a few trails that entered the woods from the school grounds and most of these were badly overgrown and seldom more than a few hundred twisting yards in length. Larkin and Tallsman searched these trails again and again. They called out: "August—where are you?—it's me," and listened to the gentle echoing of their own words. Then they'd leave the woods and search the grass that grew tall as a grown man's waist and skirted the trees and would find nothing there and would return to the woods and the voices and the silence. And would find nothing.

Tallsman said, "I give up. We're not going to find him."

"He's here," Larkin said.

"Of course he's here. But what does that mean? It means he doesn't intend to be found."

"I know he's here," Larkin said. "Come on, let's try the woods again."

Moving ahead, they entered the woods. It was nearing sunset and the trees as tall and massive as giant sentries almost succeeded in blocking the last faint rays of the departing sun. Larkin walked carefully behind Tallsman, guarding his steps with caution. It was quiet here in the woods. Larkin liked that. He was not afraid.

But he was tired. This kind of exercise was not meant for a man eighty-two years old. His feet felt as heavy as lead weights. His arms and shoulders ached and burned with each new step. But the boy was here somewhere, and he had to be found. Larkin cried: "August—where are you?—it's me."

And heard nothing.

This trail was not long. A fallen tree blocked its end like the knot at the tip of a string. Beyond the tree grass grew thick and tall.

Tallsman called out: "August—where are you?—it's me."

And heard nothing.

"Let's rest," Larkin said. "I can't move."

"All right," said Tallsman.

They went to the fallen tree and sat. Larkin was far from comfortable but the tree was better than the bare ground. The wood was old and rotten and the bark was moist from last night's rain. A slug moved in the shadows, crawling forward on its belly, cautious and slow as a scout.

Tallsman said, "Have you ever noticed? Slugs here grow bigger than snakes. It fits, doesn't it?"

"I like it here," Larkin said. "Slugs don't hurt."

"Why do you want to find him?"

Larkin shrugged. "I don't quite know. Because I don't want Milinqua to find him. I was born eighty-two years ago. I can remember when things were good. Now that they aren't good, I'm bitter about it. More than you."

"We found him together, but I still don't know. What is he? I don't know. He could have come from another world for all I know. Maybe he did."

"He didn't."

"Well?"

"Well what?"

"Well what is he?"

"How should I know?" Larkin faced Tallsman and shook his head at him, then he turned abruptly away and stared into the distant swaying branches of a faraway tree. He did not like Tallsman and never had. He had originally hired him with strong feelings of uncertainty. Now he was convinced that his feelings had been legitimate. Tallsman did not belong here. He would be happier elsewhere, at a more conventional school, at a government school for that matter. Corlin did not like him. Did anyone? Larkin thought. Yes—the children liked him. They rated him near the top every year, and once, Larkin recalled, Tallsman had topped the student poll. Four years ago. Last year he had either run third or fourth. But that wasn't him. That was the subject he taught. It was enormously popular and particularly close to Larkin's heart. He knew the subject more thoroughly and intimately than Tallsman ever would. He had lived there when it was happening.

"Are you trying to tell me you haven't any idea?"

"If there's anything I ever want to tell you, I'll tell you," Larkin said. Then he looked away. That was all. This had been a great country once. Not so many years ago, it had been a bearable country. And what was it now? Larkin blamed the war more than anything. Wars always made a country worse. But for whom? Not for those directly involved. The Canadians were claiming that the soldiers weren't real men any more. It had been years since the last time Larkin had seen a soldier. He almost believed the Canadians.

"Let's go back," he said.

Tallsman said all right and stood. He went ahead and Larkin followed him. Tallsman wanted to talk. "Don't you think it's odd that Milinqua would come here today? We found August four years ago and he's never wanted to see him before."

"That's right."

"So where has he been?"

"He's been right here. Attending school."

"Not August. I mean Milinqua."

"Everyone knows Milinqua."

"Forget it," Tallsman said.

It was very dark now. Larkin glimpsed the soft blanket of a clear night sky hanging above the grasping tips of the tallest trees. Once he tripped over a trailing vine and nearly fell but Tallsman caught him in the nick of time. After that, Larkin stepped cautiously, inspecting the ground with his toes before trusting it to receive his full weight. Tallsman walked ahead with the short solid steps of a tired man. Larkin followed.

"Listen," said Tallsman, and he stopped.

Larkin stopped too. And he listened.

"Hear that?"

"Yes," Larkin said.

"Do you understand?"

"It's not English."

"No, but I—"

"I understand too."

A voice was singing. The sound drifted lazily through the trees. The voice was lovely, singing. It sang of time, as cool as the wind, as dry as the desert. As soft and clear as a near-by whisper.

"Over here," Tallsman said. He waved at the edge of the path. "I'm going." He went, forcing his way through the underbrush. He was following the voice, but not Larkin. Larkin stood and he listened. He had never heard anything like this before. Never. As simple as that. If the voice refused to stop, if it never stopped, then Larkin would refuse to move. He would stand rooted here forever among the trees and flowers and vines and ferns. As he listened, he also heard Tallsman plunging through the forest like a haunted animal. He hated Tallsman right now, his desperate thrashing, but what could he do?

The singing stopped. *Click*—it was done. Larkin raised his fist to his mouth and bit the knuckles. He closed his eyes. When he opened them, Tallsman was standing before him. Tallsman and Melissa. He looked at the girl.

Even now in the twilight of his life, Larkin knew each of his pupils clearly in their unrestrained singularity. The day before, if asked for a description of Melissa, he would have replied: She's a small girl, not tall, but strong, with a lean firm build like a young deer. Her hair is black and cut short, close to her ears. Her features are thick and heavy, especially her mouth and lips. She is of moderate intelligence and sometimes her eyes seem to sparkle. But they don't. They twinkle.

In other words, not an exceptional child. A girl. Thirteen years old.

That was yesterday.

Today, Larkin gazed at the girl who faced him and fell helplessly in love with her. Here was a woman of true and exquisite beauty, her eyes dancing with grace, flowing with deep wisdom. A beautiful woman. Her lips parted and her voice sang words that moved as smoothly as the waters of a still lake.

"What?" said Larkin, who had not understood. His own voice seemed coarse and brutal.

"Only her," Tallsman said. "No sign of August."

"Get out of here."

"What? Where?"

"Find Corlin. Bring her to my cottage. Go to town if you have to."

Melissa said, "What's wrong, Larkin?" Her voice reached out and clutched at him. He had to struggle to separate the meaning from the song.

"Melissa. I want you to come with me to my cottage. Will you do that?"

"Yes. Of course."

"Tallsman—get out of here."

Tallsman went.

Then they were alone. Larkin took the girl by the hand and led her down the forest path. She followed compliantly, matching her step to his. He did not think of August now, for he no longer cared. Instead he thought: This is it. The moment my life has been waiting for. I have seen it now. I have seen the one who is rich and whole and full. I have seen perfection in a human being. She is the one, and she holds my hand.

They emerged from the woods. The sky was clear and cloudless, filled with distant shining stars and a shred of the moon. The silken web of the sky swept down and wrapped the cooling earth in its folds.

Melissa called on him to halt. He turned and saw that she was naked. (Had she been before?) Her body was still that of a young girl, a young deer, but something more had been added. Larkin sensed that he was gazing upon a woman so beautiful that she defied conventional description. Her beauty came from within, yet it penetrated and encompassed all of her. The moon's light caressed her, circling her breasts; it danced at her hands.

"You're worried," she said, coming forward. His hands went to her hands and she raised them to her chin. Her lips. "Oh, Larkin, I never knew it could be like this. Thank you oh thank you for everything." She kissed his fingers.

"Would you like to love me?" she asked.

He did not reply. She kissed his hands.

"Please," she said. "It would help."

"I can't," he said. He drew his hands away from her lips. "We have to go." He turned his back. He moved away toward the school.

"You're not telling the truth," she called after him.

In the darkness, he nodded. But still he went away. After a moment, she followed.

CHAPTER 8

CORLIN MC GEE:
Nine Thoughts in Soliloquy

In the darkness of the room, behind the shuttered windows, with herself, himself, and the bed. And here at her side lay Sheridan emanating that singular smell of his. Was this the smell of man? Or merely another musky stench? His legs, ripped by popping muscles, poked loosely from the bottom of the sheet that served to conceal them both. Corlin on her side, curled tightly, with her knees on her breasts and her fingers on her thighs. Corlin, who had turned her back to him so that only an odor served to verify his continuing existence. So here she was with this big strong stink and not yet sleeping.

Clark, what is it? What does this girl find in you? Haven't you ever wondered, puzzled, given it a brief measure of thought? Here—let's try. Why not? Let's see if we can find together a likely solution.

Is it your body? It's true that you're big and strong and powerful with ripping popping muscles, but is this what a girl like Corlin McGee would seek? Your cock is long and thick and wide and red at the end and sleek and slick and smooth and warm. But would this interest a woman of Corlin McGee's cultivation? Is it your warmth and comfort and gentleness? Is it your personality as slick and smooth and unlined as a paved highway? No bumps nor pits nor obstructing points. Could this be the answer, Clark? Is it that she wants someone to talk to? The exchange of thought and feeling and concept, the sharing of knowledge so valuable to any sane human being? Surely Corlin needs this too. But you, Clark? Isn't there someone else a bit more suitable? Tallsman, for example, despite his wife? Now there's a thinker, but she has asked him and he has refused. You didn't know that, did you, Clark?

If she didn't know herself, how could she expect a big slick insensitive machine like Clark Sheridan to know? Of course he didn't know, she thought, carefully lying in bed, tautly controlling the pace of her breathing. The answer, if anywhere, lay in her past conditioning. Didn't most everything lie there?

She thought back. Her eyes clamped shut, and she watched the pictures as they came, a pale shrunken face with bright sparkling eyes and clumps of white hair that shook explosively like Roman candles every time he moved his head. Here was Larkin, obediently demanding, shouting, screaming: "And then, Corlin, think. You move a foot, tickle, toe, tickle think."

"I cry," she said, eyes clamped shut, seeing the pictures, and here was a child pulling across the ground on dumpy stumpy arms.

"Cry," said Larkin.

"Oh no no," weeping like a baby. "Oh no no," body trembling, because the immensity of this grief, anger, fear, was too great for the tiny fragility of the baby's birthed body.

"Corlin, cry, please, cry, try, think—and then, and then . . ."

Nor was that all. There were many other pictures she enjoyed too. There was Larkin with his hair slicked down and parted in the middle, sitting at his big brown desk with his hands moving like forks in the air and saying, "A child cannot normally remember his first few years because he lived in a totally different world then. His senses relayed the raw data of this world to his brain, but he possessed no preconceptions with which to interpret this data. All that he had was what was actually there. So as he grows older and develops these preconceptions the memories that do not conform to his new world view are rejected, forced down so deeply that they can no longer be consciously resurrected. The world immediately past birth is dispensed with as a falsehood. But it is all there, Corlin. And beyond. That is the part where I have succeeded. By going beyond and seeing beyond. And you—"

In the bed, tonight, with the single white sheet draped across herself and himself, Corlin completed this sentence. The wind pressed gently at the shuttered windows, creeping, whisking, and her voice, speaking aloud, barely a whisper: "And you have gone farther than anyone."

I have.

But, Larkin, isn't that why you accepted me? I was your star pupil and now I'm allowed to run the sessions while you pace the school grounds, talking and laughing and patting your children in your grinning distracted fashion that they can sense and feel but not quite comprehend.

Here stood Corlin McGee's greatest obstacle. She had gone farther under Intensive Therapy than anyone before or since. When Larkin finished with her he had declared, though never aloud, that she had probably gone as far as anyone ever would. Corlin was it. She was healthy and happy and whole. She was a human being, more complete and full and real than any who had come before. This was what Larkin had told her. And she had believed him, knowing of her own ability to exist simultaneously within all lives, states of beings, planes and levels of true consciousness. All of it. And what else could there be?

So now look at her. Here she lay on the bed, this product of a great man's searching dream. If Larkin were an inventor, she might have been his steam engine, or electric light, or if he were a painter, his Mona Lisa, or a general and Waterloo, or a novelist and *A la Recherche du Temps Perdu,* or a film-maker, *Intolerance.* She was the masterwork of a genuine genius, and here she lay, wondering exactly why she bothered to go on thinking.

She could not exist alone. She needed the others. Or, just one other—that would suffice—a single person with whom she could share the vast infinity of her private universe. She was looking for love; she was. This was the answer she gave herself. Just moving along and looking for love. Pushed so far by Intensive Therapy (and it worked, it did), allowed to glimpse the way it ought to be, then returning to the real world and looking and finding it not like that at all. Therefore, she lay here. Therefore, her thighs were damp and sticky. She could not move. She was here for that.

Clark Sheridan was not the first one. That, too, was a custom of the time. To continue seeking the proper one until he was found, or you got bored with the quest, then into marriage (though most never went this far), and then into a final and ultimate sharing that proceeded inevitably toward death. But Corlin was handicapped by the fact that the object of her search was greater than anyone could hope to find, so perhaps she deliberately settled for something very much less. Like Sheridan. Not that Clark was especially awful. He wasn't, and she liked him. But his vision was dim.

And, too, he followed the customs of his time with a relentless urge toward total conformity. So twice a month at the least he traded her to his friends in exchange for whatever they had to offer. The friends expected it. Both male and female. How else was one to find the perfect mate unless one searched everywhere? And what was the need for exclusiveness? If one wanted that, then there was marriage. Right? Wasn't that the custom of this time? Of course, yes, right, and that was what marriage was for. Passed around like a fast-burning candle, poor Corlin, and she got a chance to meet the townspeople this way—Sheridan had no friends at the school—and they treated her roughly, exposing their proper contempt for Larkin and all he stood for. And it was bad, yes, getting worse, and night after night her thighs remained damp and sticky.

A sea of faces, arms and legs, mouths and lips, eyeballs rolling in a sea of pale flesh. She smiled at some, laughed at herself, watched the passing parade, the endless newsreel of memory. So why not? It meant nothing to her. It was really quite meaningless.

Not a one of them meant a thing to her.

For all of this, why not rape? Now there was an act that really diverged from the accepted customs of the time, but she knew it happened still; it happened often. A dark man looming from behind a shrouded tree, grasping at her with demanding hands, laughing, ripping her clothes. Would she scream when it happened? No—that would not help. There was no one near enough to hear her cries. Now she was running, but he caught her, cold hands at her throat like ice, weight crushing the air from her lungs, and his fingers tore at her garments, shearing off strips of light satin cloth that rose, dancing, fluttering, twisting in the night wind, his nails slashing the flesh of her arms and shoulders and back and breasts. And he looked just a little like Sheridan, but the dullness was gone from the eyes, replaced by something bitter and raging, yet sweet. And he slammed into her without prelude or wound. Or did he? Damn it, no. He did not. He drew a knife and held it to her neck. He told her either undress or I'll carve my name on your white throat. She undressed, moving slow, making him wait, taunting him, tormenting, but it was done soon. Then he told her exactly what he wanted her to do, and she did exactly that (or else), exactly as he asked, and finally began to scream, unable to bear it, because this was no better (nor worse) than the bed.

"Corlin," said a voice.

She opened her eyes to the light.

"Corlin—I'm sorry. Will you come with me?"

She patted the bed. Sheridan was gone, so she must have slept. "What do you want? Hou'd you get in here?"

Tallsman said, "Sheridan let me in. Now please. You have to come."

"Come where? And why? What is this?"

"We found Melissa. Larkin says come right away. I have my car."

"Oh, all right. But give me a minute." She got out of bed, unconsciously nude, and went to dress. Her clothes lay neatly folded on a chair. As she dressed, she became aware of Tallsman's gaze but she was also aware that her nakedness meant little to him. He was patiently waiting for her to finish and be ready. He was in a hurry; she was on his mind. So he was looking at her. That was all.

"Let's go," she said.

They went into the living room. As they passed, Sheridan smiled and waved at her. He had opened a drink and was sipping it. He lay flopped over the big red chair like a misplaced throw rug. She smiled back at him and waved. Tallsman averted his eyes, and they went out.

It was an eight-mile drive to the school and the road was thick with mud because of last night's rain. Tallsman, driving cautiously, never exceeded twenty-five. Corlin yawned and peered at the clear night sky. She looked at her watch and it was only eight o'clock. She should not have slept. She should have gone out and avoided this.

"I think it's over," she said. "The rain."

"I hope so."

"Tell me, then. When we arrive, I want to be prepared. I have to know what happened."

"Do you mean that?" Tallsman handled the car in a funny way, with both hands tightly clamped to the upper portion of the steering wheel. It seemed excessively cautious to Corlin, almost feminine, and she didn't like it.

She said, "Of course I want to hear."

"I thought you did," he said, speaking softly, pausing between words as if subjecting each sentence to a second, polishing draft. "To begin with she was beautiful. Changed—no, that's not enough—transformed. Even Larkin noticed, though he didn't notice that I noticed. It was funny. From the moment I found her crouched down beside a tree until I was driving here, it seemed like I was moving in a dream. One of those dreams splattered with thick fog that confines your every step. I could talk and move. I could even think—after a fashion—and I was fully aware of everything that occurred around me. But it was funny. I couldn't manage to take a second step. I couldn't make the events I was witnessing have any particular meaning for me. Do you understand?"

"Go on," said Corlin.

"On the way here I got the car stuck in a mudhole, driving without thinking, and I had to wait until a farmer came along in an old truck. The farmer was surprisingly friendly and he gladly helped me out. While I was with him, talking, acting, participating, everything suddenly broke free of the fog and I began to understand part of what I'd seen."

"And what had you seen?" said Corlin.

"Are you sure you really want to know?"

"Yes, and move your hands. Do something with them. Don't hold the wheel that way. It irritates me."

"Sorry." He put one hand in his lap, clenched it, then moved the other to the bottom of the wheel. "What I realized was that the important element was not what had happened. All right, here is the way it was, from an objective viewpoint: August merged himself with Melissa; for several hours the two of them occupied a single body, neither his nor hers; they went away; apparently they separated after going away; Larkin and I found her; August is still missing.

"But I don't think any of that is especially important. What's important is that a thirteen-year-old girl has become something I could never be. What am I? Don't tell me; I can answer. I am a dull middle-aged somewhat fat man who teaches small dull children the facts of a dull and dusty and ridiculously ephemeral subject. That's all. And when I first came here, I have a distinct feeling that there was more to me than that. But do you know what's really horrible? I can't remember. I have this feeling, yes, but that's as far as it goes. I know that something originally made me come here. But what? And where has it gone?

"For the past nine years I've done nothing but live my dull stagnant life. I teach my students and I fight with my wife and I argue with my children. I eat, I sleep, I fuck, I shit. Did you know that Stephanie was my second wife? Did you know that my first wife was Japanese? That she's dead? You didn't know that and yet you feel you can form judgments of me. I'd almost forgotten myself. I wouldn't mention it now, except for a lurking suspicion that it may be important.

"I used to believe that the worst thing that could happen to me was happiness. Happiness meant satisfaction and satisfaction meant complacency. I had dreams then, but what can I say now? I've seen her and she's happy; I'm miserable and I'm supposed to say that she's wrong? Now that's funny. That's hilarious."

The car pulled off the main road and moved down a winding black-top driveway which led to the main school building. The children played outside and a few of them came to the edge of the road and waved at the passing car. Corlin waved back and Tallsman clamped both hands to the wheel. Corlin wanted to tell him again to use the automatic, but it was too late now. The car went around the school building and parked behind it.

Corlin got out. Tallsman joined her. She asked, "Does he want you too?"

"I don't know," he said.

She looked at him, and suddenly all she wanted was to escape this man who insisted upon inflicting her with his pain and his suffering. Damn his problems all to hell. "I'll go alone."

Turning, she went toward the bridge. Reaching it, she crossed it, then sprinted toward the yellow light that shone from the windows of Larkin's cottage.

She ran.

CHAPTER 9

GREGORY TALLSMAN:
Servants Wept in Vain

By the time he headed back for home, it was late. He lived in a battered red frame house only a few blocks from the neat modern apartment building where Corlin and Sheridan lived, so the journey was short. He pulled into his driveway and watched peeling red paint flicker in the glow of his headlights. He turned off the lights, got out of the car, and locked the doors. Above, the sky was alive with the menace of gathering storm clouds, but it wouldn't rain now. Instead, it would wait for morning and the dawn. The clouds flocked to the moon, circled it, then swallowed it.

Plunging through the darkness, he entered his home.

Stephanie was waiting for him in the living room. She was his wife and she sat in a chair. Above her right shoulder a lamp was burning, and they had been married almost eleven years now. She was a tall woman, taller than he by a couple of inches, and very thin. Her skin was almost yellow and her hair, piled like a garden atop her head, was coal black. Her lips were narrow. Her chin snapped and shook, trembling with stifled rage.

"Are the children asleep?" he asked, crossing the room carefully. He walked as though through fire and sat on the couch. Stephanie followed him from the corners of her eyes.

"It's nearly eleven. What do you think. And where have you been?" She wore a lightweight gown piled around her hips. She pulled at a thread in one sleeve. "Do you intend to tell me?"

He shook his head. "I'm exhausted."

"And me?"

"And you?"

"How do you think I feel? Don't think I'm not exhausted. You told me you'd be home early. Perhaps by noon, you said. And here you are. And here it is past eleven."

"Did you phone the school?"

"No."

"You should have phoned the school."

"Why? They won't tell me anything."

"Oh bull, Stephanie," he said. He settled back on the couch and ran his fingers over his face, rubbed the pits of his eyes. He ought to sleep. Screw her. How could she stop him from sleeping? Let her rant. He'd fall asleep with her voice tickling his ear. "Look here." He spoke through his hands. "I'm too tired to explain now. I'll talk in the morning. Something came up at school —an emergency—and I was—"

"Was it him? Was it the spy? The child? Please don't tell me. You're involved in that. Oh no." She moved suddenly out of the chair, her gown lashing her ankles, and crossed the room. She moved like an excited cat, one hand spinning in the air, the fingers darting at his face. "Don't tell me." She stood over him.

He put his hands over his eyes. "What are you talking about?"

"I was told. You're having trouble out there. Milinqua came visiting this morning. Don't think I don't know what goes on out there. Don't think everyone in this town doesn't know. Said one of the children was the son of a known spy. They don't want to harm the child, but they do want to find the father. Your Larkin won't give him up. I've never heard anything so foolish."

The room was very hot. He was getting sleepier with each passing moment. Why wouldn't she go away and do something worth while? Wash her yellow face if nothing else. "It's not true."

"I mean it's foolish of your Larkin to risk everything—his school, his life, your career and life—for a yak. They won't harm the boy."

"There is no boy. No spy, no yak, no boy. Do you understand me? What you've heard is a lie."

"Then where have you been?"

"You don't know," he said. He dropped his hands in his lap and looked up at her. Suddenly, as he stared, the years began to peel away from her face, one after another, and soon it was eleven years ago and she was young—twenty-two—and he was six years older. Here they were talking, and her skin sparkled with the innocence of inexperience and her hands tendered his brow. They kissed. Eleven years ago.

"What don't I know?" said her voice, her youthful voice, as quick and daring as a pup.

"You don't know anything," he said, pausing, staring at her, and her smile, beaming, proved contagious, and he found that he was smiling too, and inside he was gently lighted by a glowing flame. "You don't know how wonderful you are. How beautiful. How much I care for you. I didn't realize it myself until tonight as I sat in the car and peered at the night and waited for her, but it was you not her that I really wanted to see. We were children again, and playing, and I was waiting for you to come and join me and make my life real again. She never came, the other one, but I don't care. I'm here with you now, and that's all that seems to matter. Isn't this incredible? I'd almost forgotten. Why are we here? Why are we together? Why do we share this house? We're married—that's why. And I'd almost forgotten."

She did not answer. She shook her head at him, looked at the carpet. Then her lips opened.

He moved from the couch and came to her. He took her red swollen hands in his and raised them in the air. Flesh against flesh, touching. He and she. Staring at her face, he seemed to see two faces, and one was old, and the other was new, but the new one was actually the old one. The old one was the new. It was very complicated, so he smiled and raised his lips and kissed her face. He kissed both her faces.

Then he felt himself moving again. He said, "It's going to be all right. Isn't this what you want? I know it's what I want. Working with Larkin. I've worshiped Larkin ever since I was old enough to read. Taking children who are merely children and turning them into real people. You wait—you'll see. When we get there, you'll understand. Maybe they'll let you teach too. They might. You don't have to have a certificate. It's not required. All you need is a willingness to learn. I'll make it a point to ask. That would really be wonderful, both of us together, and who knows? Maybe later our own children, too, and our grandchildren. Who knows? All I know is we've got something good waiting for us up there, and we'll be out in the country, where the air is clean and cool and where you can think and feel. Is there anything else we really need?"

She was trying to pull away from him. His grip was firm. "Let me . . . please."

"Oh. I'm sorry." Releasing her. "But—"

"I want to know where you were tonight."

"I didn't tell you? I thought—"

"No, you didn't."

He nodded. Maybe she was right. Perhaps he had forgotten to tell her. The past was gone now; in its place the present stood clear. "I was waiting outside Corlin McGee's apartment. Corlin is a teacher—"

"I know her."

"And I wanted to see her when she got back. Just wanted to see her because they wouldn't let me see. They told me I had to go away. When they needed me, they wanted me, but they never trusted me. None of them."

"What did you want to see her about?"

"About . . . about . . . I can't remember. About something."

"Oh," and she went away. She left the room and there were tears in her eyes when she passed. Tallsman shook his head.

And turned off the lamp.

Then in the darkness he sat in the chair she had vacated. Her smell lay thick around him. An odor of domesticity, but more than that. There was a hint of rot in it. A stench of vague sterility.

The house creaked as all old houses creak on dark nights with the wind blowing, and Tallsman listened to the shifting and swaying of the ceiling and walls. He was not tired now, but he was exhausted. The chair seemed to help. It seemed to soothe the aching in his back and shoulders.

He felt better now, closing his eyes. He had told her now, so perhaps things would improve. There was always a chance of that. Inside him he felt a lingering emptiness and this disturbed him. He knew this sense of emptiness was important, and he fretted. When it was filled at last, then he would sleep. So he waited. But nothing happened.

CHAPTER 10

MELISSA BRACKETT:
Sold into Egypt

They kept insisting on wanting to know the answers to the kinds of specific questions that ought not even to be spoken aloud in mixed company, but it couldn't much matter, not even to them, the way they came zinging down and slashing in like so many dive bombers, or maybe more like zipping mosquitoes, it was hard to tell, more like a batch of pesky bugs. She wasn't there anywhere. Back down instead, and sometimes she'd flop on her belly like a fishy fish, or not wondering about nothing, seeing only the inner black of dark swimming wet.

"Can't you please tell us? You're able to talk. Melissa, please. Can't you see how important this is? If they find him first . . ."

Name wasn't Melissa. Name was something else. Name was Oognotta, elsewise. Her name wasn't Corlin either, but Coalter, and why wouldn't somebody inform her of the fact? The boy came up and she couldn't immediately see him in the dark. The other voices chorused around her in their chattering but at last she detected him saying, "I'd like you to." "Oh you would? You? But you're August." "You said you would. You promised it." "But it's raining outside." "It was raining that other time too, and you said you would." It would be intriguing. With him. Why, did he even have one? There had never been a definite trace of evidence. She would soon discover, crawling out of bed, slippery sheets like ice, and those others would have plenty to chatter about tonight.

Every day is the same here. Never any change, nursing one and another. Hate them, mouths, lips, eyes. Hate oh hate. One like all the others. Here, stop. Bastard. Lifting, rising, lights in her eyes, everything light bright shine, all shine light bright glow. *This one's a girl, but all the same. Here suck your nurse's wet breast.* Crying. *Calm all right easy.*

Scampering through the mud, she dragging his hand and giggling, him just running. "Tallsman's got the watch tonight and Tallsman's a prude. He'll be coming, so I hope you're quick." "Quick?" "You come fast, but you wouldn't know yet." "Here we are." The bush ducked beneath, covering them, the smell of leaves and soil, *pitter-patter-clap-clap*. The glorious rain! She was wearing only her pajama top, her green panties, her slippers. Not too cold, so she removed the pajama top and turned so that the light from the dormitory spilled across and illuminated her breasts. "What's that?" "My titties," she said. "Oh, my breasts." Revolted by her own cuteness. Well, he made her feel dumb this way, so much like a child himself with she his teacher. "When I get bigger, they get bigger. Have you seen Watson? She's got them hanging down round her waist like inner tubes." "Will yours do that, like the tubes?" "Hope not, but they're getting bigger every week, and they hurt a little growing all the time."

She hated this old man with his twisting curling white hair dancing in clumps off his pinkly spotted head and always muttering.

"Melissa, you have to tell us. Please. Can't you talk? Joyce, you said she talked to you."

"She did. She . . ."

"Well, I think we've lost her now."

"No—here—let me try."

But he turned out pretty good. She got to like him with his every day.

"Don't you want to take these off me? And don't get them in the mud." "Why? Can't you?" The smell of rhododendron like wet inside. Dirt, and listening for pattering Tallsman, approaching, nose dragging the muck. "You don't know anything about this? You haven't ever talked with them?" "I do I do but this isn't the way I."

They moved around her, blocking the light, circling the light, and she'd have told them but she wasn't sure he wanted them to know. He was there still, down and down, taking part, listening, then explaining.

Should I tell?

Why? They won't hurt you.

Coalter is afraid.

That won't harm her.

Should I tell them that?

No.

So much different now. It was he who was the teacher and she who was the ignorant lacking pupil. But she did not mind. For the rest of this universe, as far as it was concerned, she was a teacher of great sensibility, greater perhaps than any it had ever seen before. To learn, then teach. From him, to the others.

She spoke aloud: "I am the one."

And was shocked at the abruptness of the answering outbursts. "Tell us please. You can understand. She can understand, Joyce. Make her talk." "I knew it. Tell us." "Yes, please tell us. Where is August?"

But she did not speak, for she was again down and down.

It was out now in the cold wind. "Kiss me here." "Why?" "I want you to. It makes it better." "I don't want to do that." "Oh all right but next time. Promise me next time." "Yes." "I want to see, though." He let her see, poking forward into the spilling light. Well, he had one. This was one, but it was not the same as the others she had seen so close. Twenty-four boys and three grown men. It seemed to have its own reflection. How odd, because of the light. Her thighs came open and she drew him down. Stroked his pimpled back, said, "Put it there." She stroked him down and pushed it up against her own until she was wetly sticky. Then in. "Now move . . . now . . . ah oh." But the words lacked force this time, scrunched and in. Yes, there it felt. "Move." And: "Why?"

The sky opened. The clouds withered. (It was really happening this way.) A voice stung something banging oh no she melted in and his teeth were in her mouth lips once and then coming more than she was down and down arms melting flowing what? "Let me up!" "I can't—no—this is the way." Mouth in breasts inside wetly inner tubes. *August. August.* His mind and she part of it and see twice smell and feel.

Then black.

Later Tallsman.

But she returned again to the beginning in order to know and know from the down and down.

Melissa Brackett sat silently smiling and glowing in a soft chair. Meanwhile, midnight came creeping.

CHAPTER 11

CHORUS:
Sun King

Midnight came creeping across the land, following the course of times past and present, crossing from east and west, darkening this part of the earth—*done*—then moving on to the next, never pausing, never truly finished, always westward. The island which housed the school would be one of the last places touched by the shadows of midnight before they vacated the land entirely and swept darkly across the face of the great sea, where creatures lived to whom time meant nothing, midnight or noon, all the same, and a touch of faint light brought instant death.

In the dormitory the wings were dark and the checkers stood outside thick latched wooden doors, listening, and when they heard the first tentative whisperings from beyond, they nodded their heads, for this was what they knew and expected and, satisfied, they went to their seats and sat and smiled and shuffled and began the long vigil of waiting and watching that would not end until the break of dawn.

Within the south wing of the dormitory, where the advanced students waited, the talk was concerned with the subject of life itself, with the weather and the women, the classes and the conflicts, the men and their times. One boy, seventeen years old, wanted to know why General Riley had not appeared at a public dedication ceremony in Old Washington that week. Could it be significant? Could it mean a change in the ruling structure? Another was more concerned with Gregory Tallsman's class in

Cinematic History and Technique and why the films had been
so poor the past few weeks. Another said they were actually
fairly good, if not exactly great. These were the big kids, both
boys and girls, and they talked the big talk. They were adults
concerned with issues of substance. All had been through the
most intensive of therapy, and there wasn't an unaware apple
in the whole big basket.

In the north wing, the talk was different. Here the children
leaped from their bunks the moment the lingering footsteps
padded away, and they scampered to a far corner, where a trace
of light slanted through a partially open window. One boy sat in
the center of them all. The boy was tall for his age, a little fat,
and freckled. In the dim light he waved his hands like a saint
calling upon heaven for beneficial guidance.

—If we don't want to lose it, then we've got to do something,
I'm telling you. It's strictly up to us (said the boy).

—But how can you be sure? (asked another).

—I was there, I tell you. I heard the whole damned thing.
Milinqua said he was going to arrest August, and Larkin, too,
and then the school will close, and how will you like that? You
want to go home and play with your real family? You want to go
to a government school and end up fighting the yaks?

None of them wanted any of this.

—So we're all here. We're the ones. The advanced won't help,
because they don't know August. I have some ideas, but I'd like
to hear some other opinions before I speak.

—We could turn him over.

—Who said that?

—I did.

—Are you joking?

—The school won't be closed.

—Then tell me where he is.

—How should I know?

—Because how are we going to turn him over if we don't know
where he is?

—Ah I don't know.

—Then listen to me. All of you listen. I say we've got to make a deal with them and we can't do that till we've got a good strong hand. We've got nothing they want from us except August and we don't know where he's hiding.

They all agreed with this.

—Fine. So listen to me. I say what we do is we kidnap Milinqua. I've seen his office and it won't be hard. Take him into the woods and hold him. I know a place. When they agree to issue a proclamation dropping all charges against August and Larkin, then we let him go.

—Steven, that's . . .

—Will you listen? Shut up. What do you think? I've had all day on this and I've thought it through. I know what I'm saying.

(And he did, too, or at least he was able to convince the others of this, but we won't bother listening to his plan, because it's always better to see things as they happen rather than hear first about them when they still exist only as part of the possible future.)

Outside, a rhododendron bush sat coldly beneath the faint light cast by a few stars in a misty black sky. Clouds circled and concealed the moon. The smell of approaching rain lay heavy in the air.

Beneath the bush, two children lay entwined. Both were in their late teens, and from the way they moved it was clear they were experienced at this and well known to one another. They did not speak. Their rhythms matched, their hands clasped, perhaps he murmured her name once briefly, speaking into the warm flesh of her shoulder, and perhaps he quivered once, and perhaps he moved away too quickly and too silently when it was done. She turned her eyes away from him and stared at the darkness. Then she jumped and grabbed him, clinging. She said:

—There's somebody out there. Watching us.

—No. Who? A checker?

—A boy. A lower. But he's gone now. When I saw him, he ran.

And midnight arrived, but no one noticed. Not in the white cottage across the creek, where Larkin and Corlin hammered away at their witness, who sat silently glowing in the warm light of her own blossoming beauty, who had no need to answer as she relived her life once again, and again, seeing and hearing and experiencing more and more each time. Not in town either, where Clark Sheridan prepared for bed, wondering if he ought to leave one light burning for Corlin. (He ought not.) And certainly not a few blocks farther down the road, where Mr. and Mrs. Gregory Tallsman tossed and twisted in separate beds while near by their children soundly slept, dreaming in colors of a shade and tone no longer remembered past the age of nine.

Midnight arrived, sweeping across the land like a black fire, and then drifted gently toward the beckoning sea. There it was home, and then it was gone.

Second Day

CHAPTER 12

GREGORY TALLSMAN:
Winter Sun

Sitting. And waiting. The car holding tight around him like a protective metal shield, thick and full as winter but warm inside, and the video box in the dashboard spinning pictures of leaping dancers whirling against a churning background of music and sound. *The winter sun is crying night—oh the richness deathly bright.* An old song, decadent and proscribed, but a tape that Tallsman had owned unobstructed for fifteen years. He played it now and one of the dancers gleamed abruptly nude and white. *Call the summer: all hail the light—we laugh and we die—'tis relentless but right.* He flicked a switch and the picture paused. The sound ceased, the music faded, then died. Tallsman sat alone.

The rain beat savagely against the windshield of the car. *Ram-plam-smash-blash,* said the rain. Oh, damn the rain, thought Tallsman, so where is she? But in that event, if questions were to be raised, what was he doing here? Why had he slipped from between sheets like ice to go peeping from his door (not here—not here) and then down the hallway, scraping at his beard, which obediently flaked against his pajamas, bare chest, clean suit, then outside. What was he doing, sitting in his car outside this looming apartment complex, struggling to see past a windshield splattered with the moist residue of the storm? Why all this?

Tallsman did not know. All he knew was that he had to see

her before he could hope to thrive again. Something in the way she'd moved last night. Something in the way her lips had pressed against her tongue, and then she had said he could not see her any more. They had stolen her away from him with the stark finality of a closing curtain, bodies strewn across the dim stage like bits of discarded confetti at a wedding.

Tallsman wiped at the windshield, then ducked down. She was coming at last, both of them together, but he would wait. He would wait and see her alone.

He could not see, but he knew that Sheridan and Corlin ran through the rain and dashed into his car. Tallsman waited, crouched low in the front seat, the tape hanging paused in front of him, a vast glimpse of a dancing navel. He shut his eyes and felt his teeth clashing. The other car started and his ears perked. It moved away, bumping down the slick wet highway. It was seven o'clock. He had let them get away; now he would follow. He knew where they were going. He had risen with the darkness and had moved with the first slanting hesitant light, and now it was time. Sheridan handled the wheel with Corlin at his side, and she (perhaps) put her hand in his lap, demanding comfort, but this poor insensitive man could no more provide comfort than a corpse could.

It seemed safe now. Lifting himself sufficiently, Tallsman tapped the lever that moved the car forward. The automatic was set for the school, so there was no problem there. He could barely see past the window, the rain lashing at it, painting with invisible hands rich lush designs of clear white on clear white.

He sat upright and alert in the front seat. The car ran itself, but a man was needed to guard against unforeseen dangers. There were none this morning. Not even so much as another car passing dimly through the haze. Tallsman alone with the road, except far ahead the other car, its two occupants, neither of whom was aware of the pursuing presence. Tallsman kept the speed down, and he thought:

He's out there somewhere. August. He could even be watching me right now. And what about the rain? Would the rain touch him? Would he even know it was there?

Tallsman thought not. Not August, who was greater than the storm. That much Tallsman had decided for certain while tossing a sleepless night, Stephanie breathing near by as though to draw all the available air into her lungs and leave him gasping, straining, suffocating, dying.

He watched the trees flashing past. Each flowed firmly into the next, presenting a united front of green, so that the forest as a whole was an entity but each individual tree was not. Couldn't see the forest for the trees. Or was that right? Or was it the other way around? Tallsman wondered about this, not caring, as the rain dripped off the branches and the road churned like a vast mudhole, the car spraying brown as its tires rolled unceasingly toward the school. Watching the road ahead, Tallsman saw that it was empty.

He reached the school, never once catching sight of the preceding car, but that was all right, that fitted his plans. He prodded the car and made it poke its head around the corner of the main school building, then let it rest. By leaning forward and putting his nose against the windshield he could see them clearly. Standing beside their car and talking. Sheridan's hair lay flat and slick against his head.

Then Sheridan broke away. Tallsman ducked down and put his face near the video box. Listening, he heard Sheridan pass. He waited an additional moment, then tentatively lifted his head. It looked good. It looked clear. Corlin was gone.

Leaving the car, he ran for the building. He made it, bounded a flight of stairs, and proceeded down a hallway. Here was a door of hard redwood and he knocked. A legend permanently inscribed in the wood declared:

CORLIN MC GEE—Therapist

Her voice answered his knock. "Yes? Who is it?"

"Tallsman."

"What do you want?"

"It's important."

The door opened a crack and he popped through. Inside the room, Corlin turned her back to him and went to sit at her desk.

Her face was pink and worn, coldly expressionless, and her hair hung twisted and wet at her shoulders. Her hair reminded him of the twisted clumps of brown algae frequently tossed ashore by the tides of the Sound.

The office was composed of two rooms. The back room was locked, and the front room was cold and impersonal, almost governmental in tone. There was a desk, a typewriter, a large vocorder, and several metal filing cabinets. The back room was the therapy room.

"What do you want here?"

There wasn't a chair other than the one in which she was sitting, so Tallsman crossed to the desk and sat on the edge, letting one leg dangle. Sheets of crumpled paper were sprinkled lightly across the flat surface of the desk, so he pushed a few aside and gave himself maneuvering room.

"I'm busy," she said.

"It can wait," he said. "I want to know about last night."

She looked directly at him and shrugged. "Why do you want to know?"

"I'm involved, aren't I?" he said, trying to make his voice firm.

Again she shrugged. "I suppose so, but there's really nothing to tell. She won't talk. Or she can't talk."

"But I heard her talk."

"Don't whine. I know she talked but she stopped. Joyce couldn't understand either." She smiled, looking up again, the muscles of her cheeks straining to maintain the expression. "So you see there's really nothing I can tell you."

"Oh, but there is too. It's something else. I've been thinking."

"You've also been following me. I saw your car this morning. Want to tell me why?" Now she was trying to frown.

"I wanted to see," he said.

"See what?"

"You and Sheridan."

"But that's no secret." She was impatient, angry, irritated. "Mind your own business, Tallsman."

"This is my business. Listen. Last night I was thinking. About this whole thing but especially about Milinqua. How did he happen to come here at exactly the wrong moment? August has been here for years. No one has ever shown any interest in him before. Until the night before last, he was an average kid. Well, maybe not average. But not extraordinary either. Right? And yesterday Milinqua came looking for him. Coincidence?"

"Perhaps," Corlin said, not smiling. Nor frowning. "Or fate—an act of God."

"No, not fate," said Tallsman. "Not coincidence either and certinly not God. Somebody told Milinqua what happened under that bush. That's why he came."

"That's silly."

"Why? It's the only thing that really makes sense."

"Perhaps, but who?" Her face reflected determination and common sense. She held Tallsman's attention with every word. "Only three people know about August. Right?"

"I got that far," said Tallsman.

"Well, I'm not a spy. If you think you need it, I'll give you my word of honor. And you. Are you a spy?"

"No."

"Then unless you're wrong, it has to be Dr. Larkin. Do you think it's Dr. Larkin?"

"Of course not. And stop smiling. It's not funny."

"Maybe not, but it is silly."

"Sheridan," said Tallsman.

"Oh, no," said Corlin, shaking her head mechanically from side to side. Her eyes gleamed with fierce concentration. "It's not him."

"Did you tell him?"

"I did not."

"Are you sure you didn't slip? That first morning. He came and picked you up and drove you home. This morning I saw both of you. Talking."

"Of course we—" She stopped and glared at him. Her face was drawn, haunted; but by what, by whom? thought Tallsman. Simple fatigue or sudden truth?

"Get out of my office," she said.

"If I'm right, tell me. Please, Corlin." He reached for her

but missed and slid off the desk. He stood, waiting, leaning against the edge of the wood, both legs balanced on his toes. "I have to know."

"Get out."

"Tell me."

"I don't have time," she said, calm now. "Listen to me, Tallsman, and try to use your head. It's seven-thirty and maybe it's eight. That means we have four hours to produce August and none of us knows where he is. Only Melissa knows and she won't tell us, and if we don't find him they'll close the school. Now maybe one of us is a spy, it's possible, but I don't give a damn. It's not important. Finding August is important. If you have to play detective, do something about that. But leave me alone."

"All right," he said.

"Then go."

He went. Slowly. It had not gone as he had planned, but whatever had? He had intended to tell her he loved her, but the proper moment had never come. Next time. Perhaps then. Perhaps maybe perhaps. She had asked him once, so why not again?

He stood at the door, waiting for her to speak. He couldn't see her but knew she wasn't looking at him.

He moved swiftly down the hallway. He was doing all right until he reached the point where the corridor branched. He paused there and stood with his hands hanging uselessly at his sides.

So which way now? Left—or straight ahead? Outside, the rain whipped against the bare ground—he could hear it—but outside was not for him. But where?

Standing, his head began to bob from side to side as if it were attached to his shoulders by a spring. He looked everywhere there was to look. He even looked up, and he even looked down.

But there wasn't a way.

CHAPTER 13

CORLIN MC GEE:
Princess

Corlin McGee, twenty-three years old and pretty after a fashion, sat behind her desk and watched the door slide open and a head pop through. For several seconds, Corlin McGee and the head regarded each other suspiciously. Then the head moved. It was round as a full moon, white as a morning cloud, and topped with a thatch of bristly orange hair.

"Step inside, Jennifer," said Corlin. "It's time."

"I wanted simply to ensure that you were unoccupied and quite alone," said the head.

"Yes, Jennifer, I understand. But please come in."

Entering the room, the head gently nodded. Jennifer was ten years old and thought of herself as a princess, which was why she tried to talk like a princess. Actually her position of royalty was more than a thought; in many respects, her claim was quite legitimate. She was a princess—or had been a princess—or would be a princess—or ought to be a princess. Earlier therapy sessions had clearly established this fact, and so far Jennifer had been unable to come to grips with her discovery, but she was young and this would come with time. Jennifer said, "If you please, Miss McGee. The therapy room awaits us. Already, I believe, we are somewhat tardy."

"Come," said Corlin, who went and opened the door to the back room and ushered the girl inside. Jennifer passed in a flutter of terry cloth. She wore a soiled orange bathrobe and had it buttoned around her neck so that it swirled behind like a trailing cape. Smiling at the cape, Corlin followed the girl into the room and locked the door.

The room was bare. It had always been bare, both when it had been Larkin's exclusive domain and lately for the past few years while it belonged to Corlin; there wasn't a stick of furniture in the room, not even a rug. The room as a whole measured an exact cube down to the inch. The walls were painted calm white. Originally, Corlin recalled, the walls and ceiling had been black, and later, briefly, they had been colored: one wall red, another blue, yellow, green, and the ceiling a rich flashing checkerboard of all four colors. That had not been a good idea, so Larkin had had the room painted a soothing shade of white. The floor was naked wood.

Corlin went to her place in the center of the room. Going to a corner, Jennifer stood there and put her hands over her face, concealing everything from chin to brow.

"Time was when," said Corlin. She spoke mechanically, like a recording device. How many times had she said, "Time was when"?

Jennifer said, "Time was when and I am when and back—and back back back . . ."

"And out and out and out."

"Up?"

"Deeply, deeply; thinking think. Now think see."

Jennifer stood in the corner. In front of her face her hands were quivering. The exposed skin flashed brightly red.

Corlin spoke the unlocking phrase "Jennifer, princess, declaims herself through natural laws. Repeat."

In a faraway but flowing voice, Jennifer repeated, "Jennifer, princess, declaims herself through natural laws. People trickle into the city in order to pay tribute to one who is like God. She cries to them, 'No more, no more.'"

"And the when of then?" asked Corlin.

"It is the I of I."

"The I of I," Corlin confirmed.

And it works, she reminded herself. How many times a day?

Four times, five times, as many as seven or eight? The children came to her and when they left they were greater than before. She could have uttered the phrases without thinking, and often she did. What did they do? Why did they work? How did certain combinations of words, following a single brief session of hypnosis, allow a person to open his mind and see himself truly. Nobody knew why. Nobody really knew why Intensive Therapy worked. Only that it did. At times, speaking like this, she felt like a mystic, a soothsayer, a prophet. What meaning did her words possess that she could never understand?

"Back," she said.

"To the city where I cry as the flesh of warriors deeply—"

"Farther. Back."

"No I—"

And what was it? Reincarnation? Memories of past lives? Some said this was the answer while others claimed ancestral or racial memories awakened by certain archetypal phrases. Which was the answer? Or neither? Something else entirely?

"Back to the I of the I," said Corlin.

"No! The city where I—"

"Back farther. The I of I. The when of when. *Back.*"

"*I can't. No.*"

Corlin surrendered. "Jennifer, princess, declaims herself through natural laws. Repeat."

Jennifer said softly, her hands barely trembling: "Jennifer, princess, declaims herself through natural laws."

At least she had tried, Corlin told herself, and she had not really expected to succeed. The princess was the first identity Jennifer had found and she would have to overcome the initial excitement of her discovery, made worse in this instance by the glory of royalty, before she could turn backward and seek the next one. There were many yet to find, but Jennifer was young.

Corlin was aware of more than a dozen separate identities within herself. She had even done some research, tracing her family tree back to 1655, without discovering any of her people in the flesh. All of them seemed to exist in a gray, timeless world, and none of them had anything in common with Jennifer's princess. Her people were common folk. The only thread that seemed to bind them was their uncommon plainness. Well, that, yes, but something else too. Three of her people were prostitutes, another was a homosexual, and another, a man, was a veritable Don Juan. Did this mean that these people were a product of her subconscious cravings? That was another theory which had often been raised but invariably discarded. Corlin still thought it might be right, but there was really no way of knowing. And did she really want to be a whore?

The people were not really important anyway. Discovering these hidden identities was only the elementary stage of Intensive Therapy. After them came the visions, the true enlightenment, the ability to use these people in order to help one's physical self. Or at least that was the theory. But was it really valid? She wondered. Hadn't August shown them the true futility of all their years of vain striving and struggling? Had Intensive Therapy outlived its years of usefulness? Was it anything more now than an old and broken man who refused to admit that he ought to be dead and went right on living his pointless life?

Jennifer said, "The carriage whirls down cobbled streets, the horses' hoofs clashing against the stones, and my hands waving with silver rings glowing, and a bracelet of fine rubies—or diamonds?—or emeralds?—jewels dancing and gleaming with light —and their cries for me are an ocean of sound beating breathlessly against the cold and irrevocable land."

Corlin shouted: "Back! And back! Beyond and deeply thinking! The I of I stands back!" But she knew it was hopeless. And she was tired, unable to keep her mind fixed to this trash of carriages and kings. She hoped Jennifer would kindly revert to a more interesting identity, anything other than the princess. Such as? Such as even another whore. Anything would be better than this pointless clanking down cobbled streets. And then, this morning, after only half an hour's hurried sleep, Tallsman had come rushing in to make his accusations.

Well, of couse he may have been right. She did not think so, but it was possible. After all, she had told Sheridan. She remembered clearly now. He had asked—this was in the car on the way home after that first long night—Sheridan had said, "What's wrong with you?" and she had said, "Something happened," and he had said, "Well what?" and she had said, "A hell of a mess—with August."

But that was all. He had not pressed her any further, not even taking the next obvious step. Surely he could not be the one, if there even was a one. She thought the whole idea was ridiculous. It was Tallsman's fault. If he had been able to accept the mechanisms of fate, he would have been able to understand.

Besides, he was only jealous.

Oh? Was he? Of whom? Of her? Oh hell, she thought. So why not admit it to yourself? No one else can hear. You're falling in love with Tallsman. Or, if not love, then this: he's the one person you know whom you can truly trust, and the reason you can trust him is because of his utter predictability. How nice to have a man around, knowing exactly what he'll do under any given set of circumstances. And that's why you're in love with him, Corlin. And he knows it. He's jealous.

Stop.

She stopped. And almost laughed at herself. What was she doing, for God's sake? She was doing exactly what a proponent of Intensive Therapy ought never to do. She was analyzing herself, and she almost giggled at the thought. You should never do that. According to Dr. Larkin, you either see it (and know it) or you don't see it at all, but you can never understand yourself through the processes of logic because the human personality is the most illogical of all mechanisms.

But she still thought he was jealous.

"What's wrong with you?" asked Jennifer. "Hey."

"Back," said Corlin, quickly. "Back, thinking, deeply thinking. Jennifer, princess—"

"I'm not," Jennifer said.

"You're not?"

"I'm me. What happened to you. Why weren't you listening?"

"I was thinking," Corlin said. "I'm sorry—come on." Corlin went toward the door, and Jennifer followed, moving like a small girl. She seemed irritated at the way her robe rubbed against her bare ankles.

"What are you worried about?" Jennifer asked.

Corlin went to her desk. "I didn't get enough sleep last night. That's all. I couldn't concentrate. I'm sorry."

"I understand," Jennifer said. "It's all right. I was tired of the princess anyway. I wanted to move back."

"I tried to move you," Corlin said. "But you didn't want to go."

"Oh, but I did. That was your fault. You didn't try hard enough. I'd do anything to get away from that princess. Nothing ever happens to her. And she's stupid."

"I thought you liked her."

"Dull, dull, dull," said Jennifer. "You can't imagine. The princess is like a robot. Everything here"—she flicked a hand at her cape—"and nothing here." She tapped her forehead.

"We'll try tomorrow. I promise."

"You'll be all right tomorrow? It's August, isn't it? Well, then you'll be all right tomorrow."

"Why? What do you know about August?"

"He's gone, isn't he?"

"Yes, he's gone. But why should I be worried?"

"You won't be. Not for long. In fact, if I were you, I'd forget it right now and save myself the trouble. Bye," said Jennifer, departing as smoothly as an actress. Her robe trailed ponderously after her. The door closed.

Now the room was very silent. Corlin put her chin in her hands and closed her eyes. She was thinking, analyzing herself, feasting in the joy of this new freedom. How much fun this was and what absurd conclusions she reached. The room around her was exceedingly quiet.

CHAPTER 14

JOYCE LARKIN:
Guardian at the Gate

Torn between clock and calendar, the fluid ticking hands or the rigid silent numbers, Larkin sat behind his desk with his hands neatly folded and his feet unconsciously tapping in rhythm to a top hit song of the year 1948, a good year, while outside the day had changed into something bleak and nasty which poured down rain and grayness upon the empty land below. Larkin could not help sensing that the rain was surely intended for him alone since it fed the trees and flowers and gave them life, and in turn it sought to murder him. It was an absurd thought; it was the way he felt.

The clock: the clock said nine. The clock paused briefly, cleared itself, then spoke again; the clock said five seconds after nine. The clock went tick and tock and turned and flowed. The clock went faster. It never went slower. Three hours (minus a few seconds) in which to produce the boy. Three hours in which to operate the school. Three hours in which to watch and listen to the falling rain. Three hours and then: well, that part wasn't clear. The clock said twenty-five seconds after nine. And counting.

At twenty seconds after eight, Milinqua had kindly phoned. His tight compressed official face grinned at Larkin from the viewscreen. He said, "You have only four hours left." Friendly in his greetings, Milinqua added: "We have not been able to discover this boy, my good friend Larkin, and thus it pains me greatly to deliver an ultimatum such as this, which differs in no great respect from the one that I was forced to deliver yesterday. My own feelings cry out as I speak these words. They shout; they scream. No—they cry, for you are my friend, Larkin, and as my friend, our friend, our associate, it ought to be yours to determine your own time scale, and yet my superiors are most impatient men, which is perhaps why they are who they are, and they insist upon this figure, four hours. They are the ones who say noon, and it is I who am sorry."

Thus, the clock.

But the calendar. Here was a reminder of better days. The calendar sat in the very center of Larkin's clean slick desk. There were two notes neatly scribbled upon the top page. One referred to "9" and the other to "10." There was a name after each of these numbers. After the number "9" was the name "Vegas."

There was a knock at the door.

"Come in," said Larkin, who immediately stood and pulled and smoothed his old gray suit with the starched white shirt and the red-and-white striped tie. His shoes were polished clean as glass and his cuffs were hidden beneath his sleeves and his handkerchief was primly arranged in his outer breast pocket. Always a neat man, Larkin, always a polished man. "How are you?" he said.

"Quite fine," said the woman.

"You are Mrs. Vegas?" Tilting his head, Larkin strained to see beyond the woman, but this was not easy, for the woman was huge. Larkin was not especially good at visual estimation but Mrs. Vegas appeared a good three hundred pounds. Her heavy raincoat, soaked by the rain, held to her as tightly as a blanket on a horse, and from between plump rosy cheeks her mouth peeked, and chins rolled endlessly one after another below the level of her jaw. Her arms dangled naked from her sides like twin cuts of choice beef and her hair struggled to maintain its identity in the face of such bulk.

"Dorothy Vegas," she said.

"Of course, and won't you take a chair? I'm Larkin." He indicated one of the straight-backed wooden seats and then waited tensely as Mrs. Vegas squirmed to fit herself into a safe and secure perch. She ended up tilting on the very edge of the chair, her legs serving to keep her upright while she avoided putting so much pressure on the wood that it collapsed.

"Now," said Larkin, "Mr. Vegas."

"He's dead. There is no Mr. Vegas."

"And your son?"

"Theodore. I call him Ted."

"Did you bring him with you?"

"Yes, but he's outside. In that small room."

"I may have to talk with him later."

"Certainly," she said.

"But right now I want to talk to you."

"I see."

"Good," said Larkin, putting a quick smile to his lips and using it to conceal the rapid working of his mind. He had always considered this moment the most essential of the entire process. His methods could never succeed unless only the most capable subjects were admitted. Would Theodore Vegas prove to be one of these? Now was the time to find out.

"Do you beat your son?" Larkin asked.

The woman jerked her head visibly as though searching for someone to answer this question for her. Her eyes, nearly hidden by the swollen sockets, shifted nervously, and she said, "Why, no, never."

"You have never slapped, struck, hit, spanked, or kicked the boy?"

"Why no, never."

"Why not?" asked Larkin.

The woman answered firmly. "I don't believe in hitting."

"How often does Ted masturbate?"

Again Mrs. Vegas searched the room and again she found it empty. Her voice came distantly, as though sifted through a piece of thick cloth. "Ted's too young for that."

"Now that's where you're wrong, Mrs. Vegas. Not psychologically speaking."

"I wouldn't know about that," she said.

"Of course not, and one more question—you don't mind—what is the boy's favorite game?"

Mrs. Vegas thought this one over. Finally, she said, "Couldn't you ask him? He might know better than me."

Larkin said, "I don't think that will be necessary. I'm very sorry, Mrs. Vegas, but I don't think Ted would fit here at New Morning. We have—"

"You mean you're turning him down? Like that?"

"I'm afraid so," said Larkin, lowering his eyes, studying the calendar. He dreaded this particular moment.

"You can't," she said.

Raising his eyes, Larkin jumped. The woman was looming over his desk, glaring down at him while gasping for breath with her tiny compressed mouth.

"He's been expelled," Larkin said.

"Yes," said Mrs. Vegas. Backing off a step, she wiped at her nose. "I came here."

"There isn't another school? Besides New Morning?"

"No." Her head shook vigorously. "We went to all of them and all of them said no. They're full with the others. They said go to see Larkin. Larkin has room. Try Larkin, so we came here."

"It was useless," he said, and he nearly began to apologize, explaining to her how his methods demanded a certain basic type of individual as raw material in order to work effectively and how her son did not fit this necessary mold. But he did not say any of this; he stopped himself first and said, "All right—I'll take him."

Glowing from deep within, Mrs. Vegas rubbed her eyes. "Oh —oh, thank you."

Larkin nodded without smiling and gave her directions for finding the student dormitory. She thanked him again and asked if he still wished to see the boy. Larkin said he did not think it would be necessary.

When she had gone, he studied the clock. The clock said there were fifteen minutes remaining before it was ten o'clock. Larkin knew a simple calculation would give him the exact amount of time he had remaining but he did not bother to make it. When noon came, he would know it. So why rush it along? Let time take its own time in coming.

His feet were tapping again; his hands were folded. He tried to reprove himself for accepting the Vegas boy, for allowing his emotions to interfere with his work, but he could not do that, because he knew that it no longer really mattered. The boy had been expelled from government school, and according to the law, this meant he had a period of thirty days in which to find a private school willing to accept him. If none of them were interested in adding Theodore Vegas to their enrollment—and most were already too crowded and all were too poor and acceptances were more than rare—then Theodore would find himself a member of the national army, conscripted for an indefinite term. But Larkin—good Larkin, kind Larkin, beneficial Larkin—Larkin had saved his life.

And that was all right. That had felt good. And that one other part had felt good too. Asking the questions, getting the responses, boring down to the raw basics of the matter, he had enjoyed that; it had been just like the old days. For a brief moment he had nearly forgotten everything else until abruptly reminded of the existence of a real world and then he had accepted Theodore Vegas, but he had accepted him not out of pity or remorse or feeling but simply because he had realized the simple fact that it no longer mattered one way or the other. In the past he had turned down dozens of them without batting an eye, and if necessary, he could do it again, starting tomorrow.

There was a knock at the door.

Larkin said, "Come in, please," and the door opened immediately, allowing a trio of sleek, well-groomed, smartly dressed, well-fed young people to come sweeping into the room. One of the three was a woman and she took a chair, sitting stiff and straight, while her two male companions stood nearby poised like cats. The older of the men—he was perhaps thirty—seemed a male counterpart of the woman, a clean and proud man of obvious distinction. The other was a young boy.

Larkin glanced at his calendar and said, "You must be Mr. Sarris and Miss Hartley."

"And you're Joyce Larkin," said the mother. There was a hint of breathlessness in the way she pronounced the last words: *Joyce Larkin.*

"I am. Is this your son?" Larkin asked.

The woman turned and glanced at the room as if noticing the presence of other people for the first time. Her eyes passed hurriedly over the man and finally settled on the boy. He was small, plainly quite young, and seemed to be having a problem with contact lenses. Peering straight down at the floor, his eyes were misty with tears.

"His name is Eugene," the mother said. "And today is his birthday. He's nine years old today and here we are."

"You must have been quite young."

"Do you object?"

Larkin shook his head. He said, "I assume you want—"

"Well, we had heard that you might consider. Under certain circumstances and, well, we preferred not to wait. Not that we're eager to see Eugene go—but, well, we just wanted to come and see. We agreed that it would be best for him if he spent a year here before beginning his therapy sessions. To become acquainted with you and the school, as you said in your book."

"Which book was that?" Larkin asked.

"Let me see." She laughed uneasily. "This is really embarrassing, but I don't seem to remember. But you did say it, didn't you?"

"Yes, I said it."

"I was certain you had. I've read your books the way some people used to read the Bible. In fact, that's exactly the way I feel about your work. Ever since I was a child myself. It's my Bible, my religion, and I've raised Eugene according to all your precepts. I don't see how he can fail now. I only wish I could have had his advantages. Oh, I don't mean it quite the way it sounds. What I mean is I wish I could have had the chance to come here to New Morning. I went to government school and it was horrible and all the time I was reading your books and thinking and dreaming and crying. If I had come here, I'm sure I'd be a whole other person today. Eric agrees. He went to private school but not one like here."

"You feel the same way, Mr. Sarris."

"I think this is a splendid idea," the father said, smiling toward the woman. "I've read several of your books and found them fascinating, even if you are a bit out of favor at the moment."

"We're not worried about that," Miss Hartley said. "We're ready to risk anything in order to give Eugene the best opportunity to live a full and healthy life. We're not afraid of anything."

Larkin nodded. Then he asked, "Do you ever beat the child?" Then, before the mother could reply, he waved his hand at her. "I'm sorry. Of course you don't beat him. I'm sure you wouldn't even consider the idea, and I'm sure the relationship between you and your son is perfectly and utterly healthy."

"I would like to think so," she said.

"So why bring him here?"

She said, "Well . . ." and then paused, as if the question had never occurred to her before. "Well, I guess it's because I believe in you so strongly as a person, Dr. Larkin. I think that's it. I think it's because ever since Eugene was born, even before that, even before I met Eric, always, my whole life I've been waiting for the day when I would enroll my child here. I guess that's it."

"Then forget it," said Larkin.

"What?" she said.

"I can't take him."

"But—but why?"

"I can't explain," Larkin said. "I'm sorry but there is a reason —a good one—but I cannot go into details. Instead, let me offer you some advice. If you believe in me as thoroughly as you claim, perhaps you'll take it. I hope so. My advice is simply this: if you really want your son to have a good education, then take him out of this country. Take him to Europe or go south and find him a good school and enroll him. A traditional school, I don't care. Any school. You people look like you have some money, so maybe I'm not advising you to do something that is beyond your means. If you can do it, then do it, because it's the only way he'll ever learn anything. It won't happen here in this country, and it won't happen here at New Morning."

"But—Dr. Larkin—what about the therapy?" The man had asked this. The woman seemed too stunned to speak.

"Forget the therapy," said Larkin. "It doesn't work."

They did not believe him, but he would not explain, and finally the three of them left. The whole time they had been there the boy had not once spoken. He had listened to his mother and he had listened to his father and he had listened most respectfully to Larkin. But he had never uttered a word.

Turning to the window, Larkin watched the three of them streaking through the rain, racing toward their waiting car. When they had gone, he turned back to his desk and flipped the calendar to the next page.

Above, the clock was moving. It was past ten o'clock now, well past ten, but Larkin did not notice; he had not looked at the clock. He sat, staring steadfastly ahead at the clean open air of his office, sat like a man who was waiting for nothing, like a man who had nothing for which to wait.

CHAPTER 15

GREGORY TALLSMAN:
And the Room Has Matching Eyes

The long rows of empty chairs and tables surrounding him seemed to be watching his every movement with sightless eyes and knowing expressions. He moved casually about the room, trying to ignore the objects that watched him, not wanting to give them the least measure of satisfaction, but it was not easy. He was carrying a loose roll of film in one hand, the movie he intended to show his classes today, a short film, one which would leave considerable time for classroom discussion. The film was *Zéro de Conduite*, which he normally preferred to hold until near the end of the term, but today was as good a day as any to show it. Many times in the past his classes had selected it as Greatest Film of All Time, although it wasn't, except to them. Tallsman himself preferred either *Intolerance* or *La Règle de Jeu*, but he did not really care what was considered the best and what was considered the worst. He felt people ought to like whatever it was they happened to like and to hell with everyone else.

It was only nine o'clock. He fitted the film to the projector and checked to ensure that everything was ready for the showing. Then, sitting in a near-by chair, he turned his eyes toward the blank white walls of the classroom. There was still an hour before the start of his first class and he could not think of a single way of passing the time. What he most wanted to do was think about Corlin, but he had given himself a set of strict orders earlier in the day and the strictest of all these was the

one which said he should not think about Corlin McGee. So he
had not and he would not. He was determined. Not her, nor
August, nor Sheridan, Larkin, Melissa. Not any of them or anything about them. He would go ahead with his daily affairs as
though nothing had recently happened. If no one wanted his
help, then he refused to concern himself with their difficulties.
It seemed right to him, and fitting.

But he got up and went to the door. Earlier he had heard a
soft tapping sound coming from the direction of the corridor,
and just now he heard it again. Thinking fast, he guessed
it might be Corlin knocking hesitantly at the door. She had had
plenty of time in which to reconsider her earlier words. Perhaps
she had finally realized that he was the one person here whom
she could truly trust. She had come to surrender herself to him.

He opened the door, wearing a firm expression on his face,
and it immediately fell away. There was somebody there, but
it wasn't Corlin.

Tallsman said, "Mary? Oh. Are you looking for someone,
Mary?"

The girl lifted her face toward him, but her glance drifted
past his eyes and continued aimlessly down the corridor, swept
by a current of its own direction. Her cane scraped against the
floor. She said, "It was you, Greg. I wanted to talk to you for a
minute."

"I'm free," he said. "Come in, Mary."

She started forward, using her cane to detect the width of
the door, but Tallsman moved quickly and took her free hand
and guided her into the room, found her a suitable chair, and
had her sit. After she had, he sat down beside her and smiled.

"Well, what is it, Mary?" His voice was patient.

"Some advice," she said. "I don't know if you can help."

"Go ahead and tell me," he said.

He was really quite accustomed to this sort of thing, because
in spite of what a lot of people said, he was a popular man with
his students. He felt the least he could do was be a good friend
to them, even if he could not be an especially good teacher.
Mary Rawlings was the best of his friends. She had come to

New Morning at the age of nine and now she was seventeen and ready to receive her certificate. Tallsman thought she was beautiful. Mary was hopelessly in love with him. She came to him nearly every day in need of advice, or a question to be answered, or a doubt to be cleared. Tallsman always tried to do his best for her. She trusted him and he enjoyed her company.

Mary was talking: "And I don't know much beyond that. I mean, I don't know when they're going to do it or what they're planning to do afterward. They're just worried about August and trying to help him."

"Wait," said Tallsman. "August? What are you saying about August?"

"Didn't you hear me?"

"I heard you. But before that. Before what you just said."

"I said I didn't know when they were going to do it."

"Do what?"

"Kidnap the supervisor. Like I said."

"Are you talking about Milinqua? Kidnaping Milinqua? Who wants to do that?"

"A few of the lowers. They want him to let August alone. Do you know why he won't let August alone?"

"I know," Tallsman said.

"Then maybe the whole thing is for the best."

"Maybe you'd better tell me about it," Tallsman said. "And try to begin at the beginning. Tell me everything you know."

Mary tried, but she wasn't very good at telling a story the easy way, and she started in the middle and then worked her way alternately toward both ends. Eventually, Tallsman moved in and guided her in the direction of the proper places.

What he found out was: The plot was real; it had originated with a group of lowers; they planned to kidnap Milinqua early in the day. Mary did not know exactly when. The kidnapers were led by a boy named Steven Radcliffe. Steven had overheard Milinqua say that he intended to arrest Larkin and shut down the school if August were not turned over to him by noon today. Mary had heard the story only a few hours before. At breakfast. And, no, she did not know what they planned to do afterward.

"Do you know where they plan to take him?" Tallsman asked. Mary said, "No."

"Do you know why?"

"They want Milinqua to promise to issue a proclamation absolving Larkin and August and everyone of all blame for all acts. That's exactly the way they said it. All blame for all acts. If he agrees, then they'll turn him loose. They don't plan to hurt him unless they have to."

Tallsman laughed at that, and Mary, hearing him, jerked her head.

"Are you laughing? Why are you laughing?"

"I'm not laughing at you. I'm laughing because it's so funny. I'm sorry—I really am—I'm happy you wanted to tell me about this."

"Well, I had to tell someone. And I did want your advice. That's mostly why I came. I wanted to know if you thought I ought to tell someone. Tell Larkin, so he can make them stop."

"No," Tallsman said. "I'll tell him. How's that? You probably have a class."

"There's one I've been attending lately at nine-thirty. It's a lower class but an interesting one. They read books out loud, good books usually, and I just listen. It's better than listening to a voice I don't know."

"So why don't you go ahead and go. I promise I'll take care of everything and I'll see you here at ten. I'm showing *Zéro* today. You like that one."

"I like the way they laugh at it. It must be a funny movie."

"It is," Tallsman said. "A little."

He assisted Mary to her feet and steered her toward the door. He left her in the corridor but stood and watched as, cane tapping, she moved away, walking firmly and gracefully, without a hint of hesitation in her step.

Then he went back to the room, closed the door, took a chair and propped his feet on a table. He was ready to laugh again but he didn't; he only grinned.

Kidnaping Milinqua. What a delightful idea, he thought. Why hadn't he thought of that? And when was it going to happen? he wondered. Before noon undoubtedly, which meant soon. But what good could it do? None, he thought. It might delay events an hour or two. But that was all.

He knew he ought to tell. But he had made up his mind. He wouldn't utter a word. He did not think anyone was very likely to get hurt. Milinqua was too smart a man to harm any of the children. No, nothing would happen, and if something did, if only by accident, then that would be fine.

Tallsman felt very good right now. He had not felt better in a month. Abruptly, all around him, the chairs stopped staring, and then he felt even better.

CHAPTER 16

CHORUS:
Beyond the Gates of the Tower

A building known as the Pelly Tower stood near the center of the island, looming forty-one stories above the floor of the earth, and from the roof of this building, on a clear day, it was possible to observe with the naked eye every square yard of the island's surface, and on an especially clear day brief glimpses of the distant mainland were far from impossible. There wasn't another building on the island over five stories high, so the Pelly Tower stood somewhat like a big redwood tree unexpectedly seen in the middle of a stand of dogwood.

The Offices of Local Area Supervision (Subdivision Nine—Forty-eighth State) were located on the fourteenth floor of the Pelly Tower. Unknown to nearly everyone, most of the office space on the other forty floors went unoccupied by special government decree. On the fourteenth floor, during peak afternoon shift hours, a good two hundred men and women labored at various duties, and perhaps another fifty or sixty trickled in and filtered out during the night. These people were clerks, assistants, operators, apprentices, secretaries, girls Friday, boys Thursday, understudies. There was a handful of general superintendents, numerous supervisors, and braces of specialized technicians. By actual measurements found among the original blueprints of the Pelly Tower, it was determined that the second tiniest private office on the fourteenth floor was the one currently occupied by Antonio Milinqua, for twelve years local area supervisor. The smallest private office belonged to an assistant disposal maintenance and lighting technician named David Hawks, but this was because Hawks's office was actually a storage closet and Hawks himself was in reality a janitor. Had this room been serviceable, Milinqua would undoubtedly have occupied it, for he was a cunning man, who valued the importance of anonymity.

The walls of his office were painted bleak battleship gray. There was a neon light inconspicuously located in the ceiling and a brown and green rug. On the wall directly opposite the main door was a painting, a print, which had been there the day Milinqua moved in and which he had never removed. The print, by an unknown artist, depicted a view of three animals lolling beside a still blue river which flowed through a pastoral green valley beneath a cloudless sky. To an unknowing observer, these three animals were plainly fat goats, but Milinqua insisted the goats were not goats but a mutant strain of common milk cow. Since the office belonged to Milinqua, and the painting too, public opinion soon fell into line with this theory. Mutant cows they were, lolling beside a still river which flowed through a pastoral valley beneath a cloudless sky.

There were two doors in the office. The main door (the one opposite the painting) led to a huge chamber occupied by swarms of clerks and secretaries, who chatted and clattered throughout the day, but who never managed to distract the determined supervisor from the immediacy of his endeavors. The other door, in the left wall, led to the computer room, and this was the heart of Milinqua's entire operation and a door he often used.

His desk was situated near the back wall, directly below the painting. There was a stiff-backed chair hard as nails, where he sat, and a steel filing cabinet (to the right of the desk) with three locked drawers. Two of these drawers were empty. The third held Milinqua's own Individual Personnel File, and today also contained his lunch bucket. There was a mug of hot coffee in the bucket, a jelly roll, and half of a salami sandwich. The bucket was not locked.

At this moment the office was empty. Milinqua, who had

just descended in the elevator, strolled across the sidewalk in front of the tower. He held his head down against the wind and rain, his hands stuffed deep in his pockets. The time was eleven thirty-four.

—Stop.

—What? What do you want, young man. I can—

—That's enough, Tony. See this? Know what it is? Then come along quick and quiet. It's you I want.

—This isn't—

—Maybe it isn't. But now—

—That's a toy.

—Maybe. But the bullets are real. Now that's it. That's the way.

—I remember you.

—Sure you do. That's right, Tony. And don't turn around like that again. Keep the hands still. Okay?

—I saw you in Larkin's office. Yesterday.

—You're getting bright, Tony. Now—quick—into the car. Okay now. Down on the floor. Head down. All the way. Okay.

—This is absurd.

—Move. Sure.

—But I can't . . .

—Now that's the idea.

—Trouble, Steven?

—No trouble. Tony here is an all-right guy. Let's go. No talking.

As the car rolled furiously across the green tumbling land, never moving beyond sight of the top stories of the Pelly Tower, nobody said a word. Milinqua lay on the floor in front of the back seat. He was blindfolded and gagged; his hands had been tied behind his back. Steven rode above him and there were two boys in the front seat and two girls and a boy in the rear storage compartment. The car was a stolen vehicle, although the theft would not be reported for another six hours, and it hummed gently as only the finest and newest machinery can hum.

Not far from the boundaries of New Morning school, in the

woods, there was an abandoned cabin, and a dirt road led to this cabin, but the road was so badly overgrown with weeds and flowers and grass that it was impassable by any means other than foot. Seven people walked down this road toward the cabin, drenched and soaked by the endless gray rain but exhilarating in the near-by freshness of blossoming nature. When they arrived at the cabin, six of them saw that the roof was badly cracked and the wind and rain danced and whistled and poured through a thousand holes. The walls were barely that, the floor a few rotting planks, and an old broken bed rested forlornly in the center of the room. There was a mattress on the bed, and six of the people laid the seventh atop the mattress, then removed his blindfold and gag. They left his hands tied behind his back.

The cabin was at least a hundred years old, and over the years it had housed a succession of lonely bitter men (and once, fifty years ago, two sour nasty young women). The last of these hermits, a man named Jess Wakely, had been ordered to a retirement home five years ago, and the cabin had remained empty since then. Steven knew all of this, but Milinqua, who had given the orders, did not.

—Where is this?

—On the island. In the woods.

—I know every house on the island. This one doesn't seem . . .

—Don't let it throw you, Tony. You're safe.

—What happened to the others?

—I sent them away. They're going to deliver a note so nobody worries about you. The note says we've got you and it says why.

—So Larkin thinks this will work. I am truly amazed. I would never have thought him so naïve.

—Hey, give me some credit, Tony. I'm the one who's naïve. This plan is my plan.

—But tell me why, young man. Can't you see—?

—Here, Tony, take a look at this. This is a statement I want you to sign, then I'll let you go. Look at this and maybe you'll see what this is all about. Got a pen?

(The statement was one absolving New Morning school, its

students, faculty, and administrators from all blame for all acts, past, present, and future.)

—I can't sign this.

—Well, I can't force you. But there's no hurry. We'll wait.

—Nor can you force me to stay. I've gone along with this long enough, and I'm sorry I have to be impolite and conclude the game so soon, but I really must go back to my office and attend to business. I can assure you that mind cleansing is not a pleasant operation. Nor do I think you are so foolish as to risk a murder charge. Fighting on the northern front is not a very enjoyable task either, I can promise you.

—You're threatening me.

—I'm warning you.

—I wouldn't.

The man stood and began to cross the room. He stepped carefully, walking firmly and decisively, but the condition of the floor made it necessary for him to zigzag in order to avoid the numerous holes. When the man finally reached the door, the boy raised his gun and fired a single shot. The man screamed. The bullet appeared to have struck him in the toe, for he collapsed to the floor like a deflated balloon and hugged his foot.

—You—you—

—Well, I told you I wouldn't.

Meanwhile, throughout the western portions of the North American continent, it was twelve o'clock.

Bong.

CHAPTER 17

MICHAEL ROGIRSEN:
The Whole of the Earth

The rain had made it bad at first. Oh goddamn the rain, he had hated the rain then and the way it made him forget why he was out here, but then like the gleam of a cutting knife he had seen the creek and had gone for the creek, wading in deep to his knees, then falling, then crawling, and it had not been so bad right then, because he was wet all over now like a fish, and a fish, if a fish could survive on the land, it would never have hated the rain but gloried in it, and man had originally come from the depths of the ocean, crawling out one bright day to see the sun and demand the whole of the earth, its rocks and flowers and trees and bright light sky and big moon and tiny twinkling stars and the darkness of the night. Yet still he could not remember. Why was he here? Why in the rain? Why in the creek?

He was far from the school now. The forest drew tightly around him, seeming as if at any moment the violent green might fall, crashing against the creek, covering him, crushing him, smothering his life. A reason—a reason. Why was he here? And that was all.

Oh.

The woman.

So now he remembered the woman, and with the rain rushing down his face wetter and quicker and colder than tears, he stopped, with his knees embedded in the floor of the creek and his hands raised high to the gray heavens above. It was she again, come calling to have him come running out to meet her in her resting place, where she lay waiting like a slick polished bear, like a wolf in her barren lair, and her odor reeking of the pit, waiting, this woman, but he had fooled her—oh listen—because the rain which he hated and despised and now it was the creek and the creek flowed far from the gates of her lair. He had escaped her calling, free Rogirsen man, and now his senses had fully returned and his mind was clear and sharp as a bell.

He was paused on his knees when the sound of the shot reached his ears.

Pausing further, waiting, he tried to know the shot for what it was.

It did not come again. He listened. He thought to investigate. He knew exactly where he was now. Rogirsen knew these woods better than anyone since old Jess. And that was it, he remembered. Old Jess. The shot had come from Jess's cabin. But Jess did not live there any more. Jess had gone; they had come and carried him away one winter night while Rogirsen watched. He remembered that too.

The woman. Scampering to his feet, water fleeing from him like a rabbit from a trap, he raced into the woods, for the woman had called and he had not come, so she had come for him, wanting to kill. Run, Rogirsen, flee like a bird without wings, your feet pounding like drumsticks against the deathly rot of this earth. Kick your heels on high, Rogirsen, for she follows with the wind, she is the wind, so run.

His heart was the sun at the center of his being while his lungs and mind revolved like planets around it. Rogirsen running, and he smelled, felt her pursuing breath, fell rolling, while she came on. And passed him.

Then came back. And the woods clung to him, and her, and she clung too, and his clothing shredded like autumn leaves, floating above, like dead bark on a tree, swept with the wind, and she had him where she wanted him. His eyes were dead, his hands hot as fire, and there was no way to stop her endless lunging.

But. And—but—nothing. Like nothing, like ever and before the commencement of time, nailing the man to the earth with the rain, plunging back toward the creek, throwing himself in and under, tasting blood with his slain hand.

Rogirsen waited until she had gone at last, then emerged from the creek.

August stood on the bank, saying, "Michael—I heard you."

This was the real August and, even in his shame at the act, Rogirsen was happy to see his friend. He slapped him on the arm and said, "You're wet. It's this rain. I'm wet too. Bad for all of us."

August shook his head. "You, too, Michael. Here, come with me."

"Where?"

"We'll go to your cottage and get you some clothes."

"Oh good. Somebody stole my clothes. I was trying to catch him. Thief."

"I saw him," August said.

Rogirsen grinned and slapped his friend again. "Nobody has ever seen him before. I'm glad."

"Come with me."

"It was him and not her?" August asked, as they proceeded through the deepening rain, not hating it, August dressed for winter and Rogirsen bare as a shaven cat.

"She came for me too. I thought you saw. I got away from her. Twice."

"You don't let her hurt you."

"No, but she tries, she always tries, but I get it into my mind, and it never works, and that's even worse than if it did. You can't understand because you're young. Someday you will though, August, and let me tell you it's the worst thing. They get into you and what can you do except cut off your own hand? It's not your fault—it's them doing it—but I fooled them and jumped in the creek where they couldn't get me."

"I understand."

"We never talked about this before, did we?"

They were walking quickly now and Rogirsen felt good, so he told August about the shot, how he'd first thought they were shooting at him. "But the shot came from old Jess's cabin, and

Jess was a friend, so it must have been something else. You know what it must have been, August?"

"Nothing important," said August.

Rogirsen felt better now, because she was gone and because his friend was here. After that other time, he had not known if he would ever see his friend again. That had been awful for him, because when he had a friend Rogirsen felt as if he owned the whole of the earth. Not the tiny segment of grass and dust normally allotted a single man, but the vast entire whole of it, land and sea and cloud and wind.

August said, "If you want, I can give it to you, Michael. I can give it so that it will always be yours. They'll never be able to chase you again."

They had come to the cottage standing as lonely as an orphan in the rain. They passed inside.

"How?" Rogirsen asked.

CHAPTER 18

GREGORY TALLSMAN:
Not Long for the Rain

They moved easily through the rain as though it were not a tangible reality but merely a natural metaphor for wetness, more like a coating of transparent film drawn across the slumbering earth, possessing the aura but not the substance of firm reality.

Tallsman ran ahead, drawing Corlin behind, but not running so quickly as to cause her to hurry, ignoring the streaking of his face, the fierce vitality of the wind, the pain in his eyes which moved him toward tears and combined with the rain to cut the flesh of his face deep like a razor.

As he ran, Tallsman concentrated on the woman behind, seeking to derive some meaning from this miserable running. And Stephanie. Hadn't he given her more than a chance? (He was rationalizing now.) What about last night? What had that been if not a final desperate plea for real understanding? Wasn't the substance of any marriage its natural and warm mutual sharing of the self? Hadn't Stephanie made this sharing impossible between them? And if so, didn't that make him free, his last loyalties discharged? Why could not and should not he continue to run across this land?

He felt certain he was a free man now. He had convinced himself of his own ability to seek his own will without regard for custom or tradition or what was right and what was wrong and who got hurt and who was forced to suffer.

"Quick," he said, opening the cottage door, leaping inside, and pulling Corlin after him.

She collapsed against him, out of the rain, her arms circling his back. She clutched the wet tatters of his shirt and her breath clung to his chest and her hair glided across his throat like moist leaves.

Carefully, Tallsman pushed her away.

"It looks empty," she said.

"Yes."

"Well, I was only guessing." She had recovered from the run, and now she went to look through the room. "It doesn't look like he's been here lately. I wonder where he could be in this rain. You don't see anything, do you, Greg?"

"No more than the usual mess."

"Oh, it's always a mess out here. Help me, please. Maybe they plan to come out here later."

He went to help her. Rogirsen's cottage always made him feel uncomfortable. It was such an impersonal place, despite its clutter, no warmer than a public washroom, all rotting wood and walls, no furniture except the bed, a scattering of things that were merely things: rocks and shells and dead flowers and bits of bark and blades of grass, all dead, and here a dead bird, rotted down to its bones and shiny beak, a rabbit's foot, genuine, some old clothes, wool shirts and patched overalls. Here was something. Here was a notebook. Flipping it open, Tallsman glanced through.

Nearly every page was covered with scrawls, but only an occasional word was decipherable. Tallsman read the words he could. On one page, written in huge letters, "WOMAN," and here on another page, "I . . . duck foot . . . so weekly wet." Or: "WOMAN" (again) and "augus di dnot," and there were many drawings too, but of a type that made Tallsman drop the notebook hastily to the floor without bringing its contents to Corlin's attention.

"Nothing," he said.

"Well, it was only a guess," she said. She had gone and sat on the edge of the bed. "I'm glad you told me but this was the only place on the grounds I could think of where they might have taken him."

"Mary said the woods," Tallsman said. "But I don't know where. Maybe it's all a joke."

"Oh no, I believe it. That's Steven. You forget how well I know these children. I know them better than anyone. I know them all, and I bet they've got him too. Children are master criminals because they're so much more devious than anyone anticipates."

"Steven especially."

"Yes, he'll make a great criminal," Corlin said.

"You know, he used to come to my classes every time I showed a crime picture and he'd sit in the first row and I don't think his eyes ever left the screen till the end. I think he thinks he's Bogart or James Cagney returned to life."

"You ought to get to know his other identities. But I can't tell you. Have you ever heard him talk?"

"Yes," said Tallsman. He came over and sat beside her and felt instantly warm and good. Because of the scattered impersonality of the cottage, it had already become clearly associated with her in his mind. He felt this place was more her place than the apartment where she actually lived. That place was his place, Sheridan's place, but here she was she, and him, too, and he knew he wanted her now, telling her how much he needed her right here and now but he paused, because he had remembered about her and Rogirsen a long time ago, and could it have been this very bed where they had coupled those faraway nights? He knew none of the details, but he drew away from her, repelled by a sudden vision of lean young legs wrapped around a sweating maddened waist. "WOMAN," he recalled. Of course. What other woman?

"Maybe we ought to go," Tallsman said.

"Really? But—" And she reached out to touch him.

"Can't we—?"

She jumped. "Wait—look, Greg. Look at that." Getting to her feet, she crossed the cottage, and crouching down, then reaching down, she inspected the clothes piled on the floor, pawing carefully through the garments like a prospector searching for gold. She emerged with a shirt in her hands and she shook it at his face. "This isn't his—this belongs to August. I know—I saw it that time."

"Look deeper," Tallsman advised.

Her hands moved again and this time they remained within the pile. Examining the shirt she had given him, Tallsman found it soaked with the wetness of newly fallen rain. "And not so long ago," he said.

"And here are his pants," she said, drawing them out and feeling them with her fingers. "And wet too." She stood. "That means August was here today."

"But when?" said Tallsman, standing too.

She came flat against him. His hands dropped down, rubbed the flap that dropped her blouse floating to the floor. She said, "No," and released her skirt.

"All right," Tallsman said. He was not looking at her. He was watching as her clothes mingled with those on the floor. He had forgotten the bed now. He drew her silently down and situated her across the fallen garments. He entered her immediately, knowing it would not work till the next time and wanting this done and over.

When it was all done and all over, they emerged from the cottage. The rain had eased to a trickle which dripped gently from the clouds. They walked hand in hand toward the school, which rose before them as big as a castle. It was dark now, and the clouds held the sky. The stars were far away and the moon had gone. Corlin rested her head against his shoulder. Tallsman slipped an arm around her back.

"Here comes somebody," Corlin said.

A figure was hurrying toward them, but Tallsman continued walking and refused to pause until the man reached them. He was a small man with a strangely hooked nose, which dominated his face.

"Are you Gregory Tallsman?"

"Yes, I am."

"And who is this? You are . . . ?"

"Corlin McGee."

"Then both of you are under arrest. Would you mind coming with me, please? Right away. Let's hurry."

Corlin and Tallsman went away with the man.

CHAPTER 19

CORLIN MC GEE:
If Thought Dreams Could Be Seen

He had not been so bad the first time, she thought. Promising, one might say, but not that good either. And worse now, this third time, since he had become so insistently polite, more like a butler than a lover. But she had not really expected much more from him; she could not very well demand it now. This was Tallsman, and what was Tallsman, except the man she trusted, and so what else did she really want from him?

Lying below him, she listened to the rain above, coming hard against the flat bare roof of the cottage, then soft, then softer. The rain, too, was dying with the end of the day, and perhaps when they finally stepped outside, they would find the rain gone and the sky wiped clean and bright and looking new and shiny as an apple. But she did not think so. It was way past noon now, and if the men were not here already, they would soon be coming. With Milinqua, or without Milinqua? Now that was something she would be interested in seeing—eventually—but it did not seem to matter very much right this instant. How much better to wait patiently in the arms of this man, her trusting lover, pulsing when he pulsed, moaning every few seconds, twisting just so, and legs raised, lowered, around and around, all that was expected of her as a woman in terms of harmony and grace and rhythm. Oh but she was good at this, so wonderfully delightful, so practiced and experienced, and they might get tired of Larkin and then come looking for the two of them and come peeking here and see and roll him off and what a laugh. They would not say no, of course. Men like them had witnessed such flagrant immorality as to make an adulterer seem no worse than a juvenile bubble gum thief. So the man was bored with his wife (it could happen) and so the woman led him on (it happened all the time) and so they went to bed together (so what?). That wasn't any crime; it barely qualified as a minor tragedy.

Ah, but she was dead down below. Her thighs were a graveyard of deceased sensations. She had more feeling in the pits of her elbows than down below. Maybe let him have an elbow. What a rare and shocking treat for him. Oh, too slow, she realized; he had been up there too long. Her eyes were closed and pulsing patterns of blue and green thundered across the backs of her lids. It had gone on too long. She was almost beginning to sense a vague tingling down around the graveyard, and that would never do. Like a feather tickling her nose. And a gentle pressure. Her eyes were closed—let's see:

Clark?

Oh Clark dearest yes oh yes.

No, not Clark. She could not trust Clark and he was hardly an improvement over Tallsman. Rougher perhaps, minimumly brutal, and sometimes with him she felt a sensation (like an extra big feather) down there.

But no, not Clark.

So who else? There wasn't anyone else.

That was her problem. This time was not her time and that was all there was to it. Why couldn't she have been born eighty years ago? Or eighty years from now? The customs of this time were not in tune with the spiritual needs of her soul, so here she was, not much past twenty, and all used up, dead down below in the one place where it was important to stay undead. What she needed was a man, one man, the right man, like in 1924, then she would be fine. The graveyard would bloom like a garden and the roses would flourish like wild grass and the rhododendrons would blossom and mingle with the swaying tulips. She had half thought Tallsman might be the one man she needed, but he was too old, too wasted, too self-involved. He had done his yak and then his wife, and there wasn't enough left for her. She liked him, of course, and she trusted him, but that wasn't nearly enough for a woman with her needs. She needed more, much more, and this was an important moment for him, and she was positive that by the end he would think it had gone well. And perhaps it had. She whispered something in his ear and snapped like a whip. And she? And Rogirsen?

Michael, she thought, but not passionately, for that had long ago been purged from her system. No. She thought of Rogirsen mingling and merging and absorbed by August, with his dark haunted eyes suddenly burning brightly with enlightenment, just like Melissa, and moving her head awkwardly against the floor, she wondered what it would be like.

Michael, when it's done and you're whole again, come and tell me and let me see that light burning in your eyes like a star gone haywire. Come and share that much with me.

As they walked across the grounds, the three of them approaching the school, Corlin turned to the man with the hooked nose and said, "You were looking for us earlier, I imagine, and you didn't know where to find us. See that cottage back there. That's where we were. Just us. Me and him. Nobody else."

"All right," said the man.

She smiled, knowing now that her original feelings had been right; the man did not care. "We were committing adultery," she said. "This man—he's married. He's also a teacher here at the school."

"Is that so?" the man said.

Tallsman grabbed at her arm, but she jerked away, and then they passed inside the school and it was dark here and she could not see the man's face.

He took them to Larkin's office and held the door while they passed inside. He did not come after them. There were four people in the room: Larkin and Melissa and two men who looked as though they were in charge. Both of these men were standing. One was a black man with broad shoulders and a chest as big as a boat and the other was a short white man with quick skipping eyes. Larkin was sitting behind his desk and Melissa occupied a chair at his side. Larkin's expression was dark and tragic. Melissa glowed like a burning fire.

The black man spoke: "Miss McGee?"

"Yes?"

"My name is Rutgers. I'm an assistant to the local area supervisor and this is Barney Ford, who is another assistant. We'd like to ask you some questions about this man August."

"Boy," said Larkin. "He's not yet thirteen."

"Yes, a boy," Rutgers said. "A child." He turned back to Corlin. "We've been looking for him and haven't found a trace. Dr. Larkin has been helping us, but we understand that you have some information that may be of some assistance to us in our search."

"You're with the supervisor?" Corlin said. "Why isn't he here?"

"What?" said the man named Ford. He glared at her.

"Where's Milinqua?" Corlin said.

Larkin shook his head at her, but Rutgers merely grinned and shrugged. "Somebody has kidnaped Mr. Milinqua," he said calmly, as though this were a daily occurrence. "Some of your children, I understand. Do you know anything about it?"

"Of course not. I haven't left the grounds all day."

"We know," Rutgers said. "We checked."

"You're very competent," Corlin said. She turned and studied Melissa, who sat primly beside Larkin's desk, her hands clasped in her lap, her legs demurely crossed at the ankles. But her eyes were far away. The same as they had been the night before. Corlin was beginning to wonder if Melissa would ever return to the earth again, or would she continue to wander forever among the distant stars? Was this the meaning of enlightenment? Would Rogirsen, returning, be like this too?

"Would you mind doing us a big favor?" Rutgers asked.

"Of course not," Corlin said.

"This girl here. We understand the boy attacked her and did something to make her like she is now. We've been trying to ask her some questions but it seems pretty hopeless. Dr. Larkin tried and he couldn't get anywhere either. We were wondering if—"

"I'll try," Corlin said. She went over to Melissa and stood in front of her. "Melissa? It's me—Corlin. Can you understand me?"

Melissa sat still. Briefly, her eyes seemed to flicker and move. But there was no understanding there.

"Melissa?" said Corlin again.

No response.

"This is useless," she told Rutgers. "We tried all last night, wanting to find August. She didn't say a word."

"She sang to me," Larkin said. "But that was earlier."

"I heard her, too," Tallsman said, from the back of the room.

"And who are you?" Rutgers asked, frowning. "What do you want here?"

"I'm under arrest. I'm Gregory Tallsman. I'm a teacher here."

"He was the one with me when I found the girl," Larkin said.

"Then maybe he knows something," said Barney Ford. "Do you know something?" he asked Tallsman.

"No," said Tallsman, shaking his head. He smiled lightly. "I wish I did, but Dr. Larkin knows everything I know and I'm sure he's told you."

"Do you have a wife?" Ford said.

"I do."

"And children?"

"Two."

"Would you like to see them in the army?"

Tallsman shook his head wordlessly.

"Then you'd better start telling us what you know."

"But I don't know anything."

"He won't talk," Ford told Rutgers.

"Oh," said Rutgers. "He won't, will he? Then you can go, Mr. Tallsman. Since you won't talk. But please don't stray. We may want you later."

"I won't," Tallsman said. His face was flushed red and he looked angry. But he went.

"I knew he didn't know anything," Ford said, after Tallsman had left. "But I felt I had to make sure."

"We've already provided Dr. Larkin the facts in this case. But perhaps you would like to hear them too." Rutgers was talking to Corlin. "This boy, August, have you ever wondered what he is, where he came from?"

"I have."

"And I can tell you. He's not from here. He's an enemy agent. Deliberately inserted here in your school in order to subvert this part of the world. In fact, he's really more than an agent; he's a weapon."

"I'm afraid I don't understand," Corlin said.

Larkin answered: "They say August is a deliberate biological mutation, something cooked up in the enemy laboratories and placed here. They say he's like a time bomb and now he's exploded. They say he takes people like Melissa and makes zombies out of them. It's horrible, they say."

"But Melissa isn't a zombie," Corlin said.

"Then what is she?" Rutgers said.

"I don't know—but she's not that. She's thinking."

"That's what they want you to believe," Ford said. "I know how the yaks think. It's all subversion. All of it. If Milinqua were here, he could explain it."

Larkin nodded his head in careful agreement. Corlin looked at him and frowned. He had both hands clasped across his chest so firmly that she was afraid he would tear his shirt. What had these men done to him? Or was he only pretending?

"May I go now?" Corlin said.

"Not yet," said Rutgers. "You're still under arrest."

"But there's nothing more I can tell you."

"But there is. You haven't told us a thing about the kidnaping. We understand you are the one who masterminded the entire plot. We'd like to have Mr. Milinqua returned to us. We really would."

"This is ridiculous. I never heard of this until five minutes ago."

"Not according to Dr. Larkin. He says you were the one and we believe him."

"Joyce," said Corlin. "Why?"

"Trying to cooperate, Corlin. I suggest you do the same. These men won't harm you if you tell them the truth."

"Of course not," said Rutgers. "Now—shall we begin at the beginning?"

They began at the beginning. Corlin stood, listening, answering, watching the night moving past like a slow-motion film, each individual frame of action clearly defined and distinct. She answered all of their questions as well as she could but it was not enough. She knew nothing of the kidnaping, except what Tallsman had told her, but they would not believe her. Larkin sat like a gargoyle behind his desk, never speaking, seldom moving. After a few hours, two men entered the office and took Melissa away with them.

Corlin began to lose faith. Would this ever end? The same questions were asked again and again. Rutgers was polite and kindly, like a big brother; Ford hurled veiled threats behind every word he spoke. Then she saw a solution. It was coming toward her, streaking across the land. She could see it clearly now. It was a man tearing at the forest as he ran, ripping trees from the ground and snapping them like twigs in his bare hands. It was Rogirsen, coming to her rescue.

It was almost midnight when Rutgers said, "I think she may be telling us the truth."

And Rogirsen continued to run.

CHAPTER 20

GREGORY TALLSMAN:
The Growth of Poison

It had stopped raining.

As he marched down the corridor, Tallsman had listened to the rain beating steadily against the roof. There was a man lounging easily outside the door of Larkin's office and the man had called: "Hey—don't try to go too far," but Tallsman had kept walking, listening to the familiar even pattern of the rain: *pitter-patter-slap-slap.*

Tallsman had listened to the rain, striding firmly and decisively, like a man certain of his mission.

But when he reached the outside, he discovered that it had stopped raining.

Turning his eyes to the sky, Tallsman watched as the clouds opened as though parted by a sword and the moon whirled down from where it had rested to resume its proper place in the center of the sky. The stars unfurled around the moon like an escort of glittering guards, and Tallsman thought, *Poor Corlin—poor girl,* and walked into the darkness.

He was not angry now. The night was too precious to be marred by bitterness. There was a woman who was in love with him, a woman who held him in her arms and whispered against his lips, and he knew he had to feel fine, wonderful; he was far from being angry.

Inhaling, he tasted the night air. It seemed heavily laden with dark conflicting emotions. Out here somewhere in the night was August, and with him was Rogirsen, and somewhere else

Milinqua sat surrounded by his keepers. Everything seemed so utterly chaotic, so thoroughly meaningless, that Tallsman nearly laughed aloud. Or cried. But nothing would help, and the air was clean and sweet and felt like a brand-new morning pressing gently against the pores of his face.

Once he paused and turned to face the school building. He was surprised to see two lights burning. One came from Larkin's office, but the other emanated from far to one side of the building. Without thought or expectation, Tallsman turned and walked that way.

Still without expectation, he arrived and opened a door and squinted his eyes against the stark light. A smell reached him, an odor of stagnation and labor, hot days and long nights. He knew where he was. The school gymnasium.

And there was Sheridan down at the far end of the floor. Tallsman called out, "Hey! Sheridan! Hey!" and hurried toward the man.

Greeting him with a smile, Sheridan asked: "Have you seen Corlin?"

"She's with Larkin—in his office."

"That's good. I thought she was here. I'm leaving soon and I can take her home. I was fixing some of this equipment. I think I'm the only one here who can do it."

"She won't want to."

"Won't want to what?"

"Ride home with you. She's under arrest."

"Oh," said Sheridan. Shaking his head, he stepped close to Tallsman. "What happened?"

"August."

"What about him?"

"You know. They came here looking for him. They think she knows where he is. But she doesn't."

"What do they want with him? He's only a kid."

"Didn't Corlin tell you?"

Sheridan appeared to think, but he said, "Not that I can remember." Tallsman wished he had chosen another location for this confrontation besides the gymnasium. He did not like this place and he normally avoided it. These were Sheridan's home grounds. The gymnastic equipment—the ropes and bars and mats —the basketball court itself—the balls and rackets and other equipment strewn across the floor—the smell of perspiration—all of these things belonged to Sheridan. These were part of him. Tallsman was the odd man here.

"You told them about her," Tallsman said. "I know it was you."

"What do you mean?" Sheridan said.

"I mean you turned her in. I know it."

"But I didn't," Sheridan said. "I don't even know what you're talking about. I've never had anything to do with August. He doesn't like sports and I don't like him. He doesn't know how to enjoy himself. You know, I don't think I've ever seen him smile." As he spoke, he reached down and picked a stray basketball off the floor. He dribbled it skillfully, switching easily from hand to hand, and when he finished speaking he tossed the ball casually into the air. It rose a few feet, then came down, and Sheridan caught it on the tip of one finger, where it continued to spin and spin.

Tallsman, watching the whirling ball, round and round, said, "Well, maybe I'm wrong."

"I think you are." Sheridan allowed the ball to hit the floor, bouncing once, then rolling forlornly toward a distant corner. "You've got the wrong man."

"I better go," Tallsman said.

"Stay if you want. Play with my toys. I'm going soon myself."

"That's all right."

"And if you run into Corlin, tell her where I am. I wouldn't worry about her. Things will work out. I'm sure it's all a mistake. Anyone can make them, you know."

"Sure," said Tallsman.

He passed into the outer darkness, which gripped him briefly, held him momentarily, but then he pushed away, escaping its clutches, and moved forward. He told himself that it did not matter about Sheridan. Nothing mattered, he thought. It was better to swim with the current and forego all speculation.

He continued to walk, but without any clear destination in mind. He was walking and that was sufficient for the moment. The evening air wiped at his face, tickling his nostrils, freeing him from the taint of the gymnasium. He was back in his own world now and that was better. He passed the school, where a light still burned in Larkin's office, and moved onward, settling back, letting his feet carry him.

His feet carried him to Rogirsen's cottage, but that was all right. He approached and saw that a light was burning from within. Now how could that be? But he did not stop. His feet still ruled his body, and they made him move faster, quicker. Probably one of Milinqua's men, he decided. There were a lot of them around the school tonight. But that was all right too. He was not afraid of them. He had told them the truth.

Maybe it was Corlin. That was possible, he decided. They had released her and she had come straight to this place where she had known him best. But should he go to her now? Should he wait? Did she want to see him? Did he want to see her?

His feet reached the door and his hand went straight into the air and his knuckles rapped.

The door opened.

It was Rogirsen.

"You're here," Tallsman said. Then he stopped and studied the man but he could detect no obvious changes, so he slipped past him and entered the cottage. The door closed behind him and he whirled.

"Yes," said Rogirsen. His voice had not changed. "You and she were here before," he said. No. His voice had changed. It was softer than before and there was a quality missing. A sense of hysterical intensity which had always lurked slightly beneath the surface of his voice, even when he was making the most commonplace statements. That was gone now.

"What do you know?" Tallsman asked.

"I saw you," Rogirsen said.

"How?"

Rogirsen shook his hands in front of him, then lowered his

gaze and looked at his hands. "There isn't time to talk. You have to come with me." He spoke as calmly as a saint.

"Why?"

"There are people you must see."

"Who? Not August?"

"August is gone. You must come with me."

"I can't. I'm under arrest." He started to explain what had happened but Rogirsen's hands were trembling violently like two trees in a storm. Tallsman stopped and said, "All right—I'll go."

"The woods," Rogirsen said.

"Yes. All right. The woods."

Together, they left the cottage and Rogirsen led him down toward the creek and they followed its twisting path away from the school and into the darkness of the woods, where neither man spoke, watching the water instead, first as it sparkled with the light of the moon and then as it turned black, dark as a world of shadows, and still they followed the water.

CHAPTER 21

MICHAEL ROGIRSEN:
One Plus One and One

Rogirsen and Tallsman followed the path of the creek through the woods.

The creek was bubbling, flowing, near and the fish were crying (Rogirsen heard them) insistent and loud. For so many years he had listened to these fish, and now for the first time he was able to understand why they were crying, and it came as a shock, learning the fish were merely celebrating the coming of the rain, for the rain meant life to them, new water come to join and mingle with the old.

Rogirsen walked, stumbling in the darkness, beside the flowing stream, ignoring the man who walked behind him, dominated by his own internal contradictions, which left no time for those of another. Who was this other man, anyway? It wasn't August, the one who had pretended friendship and then refused to listen when he repeated, *I can't I can't it's wrong*, not even explaining why it was not wrong, merely forcing him (for his own good) with an incredible strength far greater than those others who had forced him to follow their whims in the past. But maybe this time was the one time when what they said was good for him turned out to be good for him. He did not know yet. But he wanted to know.

Reassure him, said the voice in his head.

Who? asked Rogirsen.

Tallsman. Tell him it's important and tell him he won't be harmed. He's afraid.

I'll tell Tallsman.

Yes, said the voice, *tell him now.*

Peering past his shoulder, squinting in the dark, Rogirsen glimpsed Tallsman's form struggling beside the black water. He said, "This is important."

"Who?" said Tallsman. "What's that? Oh. Well, it had better be important. But you say it's not August. I want to find August. You must know where he is."

"Nothing will harm you," Rogirsen said.

He thought: Perhaps all of this is part of some larger pattern, one I cannot yet understand fully. That could be. And Rogirsen could not help reviving this thought as he walked beside the chattering fish, the bubbling swirling water. He thought that the water might be a part of this pattern. Perhaps the water was merely an invention of the man (Larkin) and the woman (Corlin). Perhaps there was no creek. And the voice in his head. That too was undoubtedly part of the pattern. An implanted device designed to observe and control his thoughts. And Tallsman behind him. That part was very good, but he understood now. Tallsman was—

Listen to the earth, the voice told him.

I won't.

Do it—listen.

I can't.

You can. Listen. Can't you hear the earth?

Rogirsen listened and he heard the earth. He heard it shaking and trembling beneath his feet. He knew that the earth was happy, and for a moment he regretted the necessity of so harshly treading upon its surface. But no, the voice told him that was wrong, for what reason could there be for the existence of this dirt and mud and rock except as a carpet for the feet of mankind? These thoughts were not his thoughts. He sensed this. He tried to drive them away. But he could not; they would not go. They stayed, dominating.

Tallsman said, "How far is this place? Wherever it is we're going. There's nothing here except trees and it's so dark I can't even see my hands."

"I—" said Rogirsen.

Tell him about the cabin.

"There's a cabin."

"Here?—where?"

"My friend lives there."

"What friend? August?"

Tell him to wait.

"Wait," Rogirsen said. "It's not far from here."

The two men continued their awkward stumbling journey through the darkness, and now the trees seemed to lean downward, tilting, clutching, grasping. Rogirsen could remember when, walking here, he had seen these branches as grasping hands and the leaves as eager beckoning fingers. But he knew better now; he knew that this was not so. Trees were trees and branches were branches and leaves were leaves. The voice had told him this, and now he recognized the voice. It was his own.

And it was helping him.

For the first time he listened to the voice because he wanted to listen, and the voice told him many things he should have known. It told him that Larkin meant him no harm and the woman even less. Larkin had thought of him as an object, a convenient tool, and when the tool had broken, he had forgotten to take the time to fix it. But that was all.

The voice told him many other things, and it also told him he was coming near.

Rogirsen waved to Tallsman, then touched his arm. He pointed into the woods and the two men went that way. It was a short walk down a deep path. Soon, the cabin came into view and the moon appeared and the trees were gone. The cabin sparkled with light.

"What now?" Tallsman asked.

Go forward, the voice said.

Rogirsen ignored the voice. He already knew. "Come on," he told Tallsman, and they went ahead.

CHAPTER 22

CHORUS:
Birthday

Loosely jammed inside the cracked stem of an old beer bottle (found outside the cabin near the bottom of an otherwise useless pile of rubbish), the small candle provided the interior of the cabin with a dim and flickering light. The corners of the room were dark, and the ceiling above was invisible behind a heavy black haze. Only the faces were clearly illuminated. The five poised faces which rested near the candle's flame. Five faces; five people.

One of the five was Antonio Milinqua. His foot hurt dreadfully and he had lost all conception of true time. He knew he had been waiting here in this cabin for a long time, and he knew that he did not greatly mind. This imprisonment was nothing more than a mild irritant, and it was that only because there was work at the office and, come morning, he would have to work especially hard at various routine administrative matters. It wasn't the difficulty of this work which irritated him, but the hastiness the necessity of catching up would require. Milinqua despised hastiness in all its myriad forms; he was a naturally careful man.

The other four faces belonged to the children. Of them, only one (Steven) was especially noteworthy, and this was because he was holding a gun tightly in one hand. He was no longer worried that Milinqua might try to escape, because earlier in the evening he had confirmed to his satisfaction that Milinqua could no longer walk, but he happened to enjoy the feel of the gun. The other children were not important. Their presence here at this moment was purely happenstance. Any one of them could easily have been another and nothing would have changed. The children were people. They talked and acted the same as all people talk and act.

—The time? (Milinqua asked).

—I think it's around nine. Why? Are you ready to sign?

—You ought to know by now that that is impossible. Why do you keep asking me? Have you forgotten who I am? I am merely a pawn in this game. If I sign your statement, I will be relinquishing my right to remain on the board. I do not wish to do that.

—Would you rather die?

—I see no difference. I am truly very sorry. I wish you no harm. Dr. Larkin is my friend. But I cannot sign your statement. Instead, I worry about you.

—About me? Why?

—My foot. It is dangerous. Infection, gangrene, a disease. All are possibilities. If I were to die . . . well, I would not want to be in your position.

—Then sign the statement. Save my life that way.

They had eaten earlier, around dusk, splitting a can of cold beans five ways. The children were accustomed to finer meals, but the one day's change in diet was acceptable to them. Milinqua welcomed the beans. They reminded him of home when he was a boy. A can of cold beans had been a frequent meal then, and he and his family had lived in a one-room cabin very much like this one. Milinqua ate slowly, dreaming of the past.

—Steven, I'm cold (said one of the children).

—Then move over by the fire.

—That candle? You call that a fire?

—Then put on a sweater. Do something. Go home.

—Well, you said this was going to be fun.

—I'm having fun.

—But we're not. You got to shoot him in the foot. No wonder. We didn't even get to see it.

—I'll tell you what. If he hasn't signed by morning, I'll let you shoot him in the other foot. How's that sound? Now shut up and wait.

Of the four children, two were girls. Both were pretty, although one was much prettier than the other. It was this prettier girl who had complained of the boredom. The other, not so pretty now, was certain to be a beautiful woman in a few years. She had the round saucer eyes, the high tilting forehead, the misshapen bent mouth that beautiful women often have when they are children. Her name was Lorcas; the other girl's name was Lynda. Milinqua noted these various facts, because the noting of facts was an important element in his work, and Milinqua always performed his work very well.

—Why don't we try to get some sleep? Somebody'll have to watch, so I'll watch first.

—I'm too cold to sleep.

—Well, if he'd just sign—

—I cannot sign. I am really very sorry. I wish you could understand my point of view.

Outside:

Passing through a tiny hole in the wall of the cabin. Leaping past the clearing, dashing between the trees, fumbling through the deep forest. Here stood August, watching the cabin. He stood, listening to the voices. He heard everything and he saw everything. He was five hundred yards from the cabin. Between him and it stood a solid wall of giant trees, but he saw past them and over them as easily as if they had been made of polished glass.

He moved forward, approaching the cabin, not hurrying. He came close, glimpsing the dim light, but he did not hurry. He walked as calmly as an aged gentleman out for an afternoon stroll.

—There's someone coming.

—No. Who? Down the road?

—From the woods. I saw a shape. Moving.

—An animal?

—No. Not that big. Not here.

—Then who? I wonder who.

Before reaching the cabin, August paused and shouted his name. From within the cabin, the children answered him. He went ahead and passed through the door and made his way into the cabin, standing in the light. Steven came forward to greet him.

Trembling with fear, Milinqua looked at the boy. He heard the children expressing their joy and delight. Here was their hero, but here, too, was his fear. What was this? What had they set loose on an unknowing world? This was no boy. Milinqua shook like a small child trapped in a nightmare.

—They haven't convinced you, Mr. Milinqua (said August).

—No. Not at all. (Calm, stay calm, he thought.)

—But you appear to be trembling. Are you cold?

—A little.

—We'll get you a blanket.

—Thank you.

August turned toward the children and studied each in turn.

—You. What's your name?

—Lynda. Don't you remember me? You used to sleep next to me.

—I remember. And you. Your name.

He asked the others their names and they told him. The candle flared, faded, nearly perished. In the encroaching darkness, Milinqua trembled alone. And waited.

CHAPTER 23

GREGORY TALLSMAN:
The Coronation of a Bishop

What amazed him was the fact that he was not amazed. The sky lay distantly invisible above the trees. It was dark here beside the creek and Tallsman could see only a few vague shapes. The stream, wide and black, was flowing near. He heard the water moving but he could not see it. When he tried to walk cautiously, aware of the darkness around him, he would trip and stumble and nearly fall, but when he walked without thinking, as casual as a man out for a stroll on a bright day, then he had no trouble.

But he didn't know where he was going, and this bothered him. Rogirsen led and he followed. He could not see the other man but he could hear his footsteps treading evenly in front of him and he followed the sound.

"How far?" he asked, at one point.

"I don't know."

"But you know where we're going?"

"Nothing will harm you."

Rogirsen had changed but Tallsman did not feel safe with him. His transformation was not so apparent as Melissa's, but the changes had surely occurred. Rogirsen had found August and had been taken by August and here was the result. Following, Tallsman wondered: How many others? Where will it end? Or will it ever end? Or should it?

"I'd still like to know where we're going," Tallsman said. "And why. I'm not supposed to leave the school. I'm taking a big risk."

"Nothing will harm you."

"You've told me that a hundred times. Can't you say anything else?"

Rogirsen said nothing.

"Well, what about August? Where is he? You have to know."

Rogirsen said, "Wait—I think—"

Tallsman stopped and waited. He sensed Rogirsen standing a few yards in front of him.

Then Rogirsen said, "This way," and Tallsman felt him turn sharply toward the woods. Tallsman followed, passing between closely set trees, tall as giants but barely visible. After a moment, they emerged from beneath the thickest of the trees and saw the sky again. The light was better here and Tallsman glimpsed his own arms swinging at his sides. There was a trail of sorts here and they turned to follow it. The trail was badly overgrown with blackberry bushes and fallen branches, but it was passable.

Soon, Tallsman felt their destination drawing near. He slowed his pace and stared ahead and then he saw it. The cabin sat in the center of a narrow clearing. There was a light burning inside the cabin and faint luminous rays slipped through the cracked walls in a dozen places.

"This is it," Rogirsen said.

"Yes. Well, now what? Do we go inside?"

"Yes—go," Rogirsen said.

Tallsman waited a moment, but Rogirsen did not move. Then, with a shrug, Tallsman stepped past the other man and went forward. He entered the cabin through the largest and widest hole. The interior was dim, almost dark, but after a moment he could see clearly. He saw a candle burning like the last burst of a dying sun, propped in the cracked stem of an old beer bottle. There was no other light. Leaves and branches covered the floor in a makeshift carpet. There was an overturned bed leaning against one wall, but no other furniture.

Tallsman stepped toward the bed and peered behind it. August was there.

He said, "August."

There was no reply. Tallsman reached down and gave the boy a shake. He seemed to be asleep but his flesh was cold to the touch. His breathing was loud and regular. Tallsman went back to the doorway.

He shouted: "Rogirsen! Come here!" and waited while a shape extracted itself from the surrounding shadows and came toward him.

"August is here," Tallsman said.

"Yes."

"But he's asleep. Or sick. I can't wake him."

"Yes."

"What should we do?"

"Take him away," Rogirsen said. "It's cold here."

Tallsman nodded and the two men went into the cabin. Rogirsen took the boy in his arms and carried him outside. He said, "We'll take him home with us."

Tallsman followed. The two men retraced their steps through the woods, down to the banks of the creek, then along the creek. The walk seemed shorter this time. When they reached the school, they moved away from the creek and headed toward the main building. They walked cautiously, Rogirsen still carrying the boy, and Tallsman constantly peered at the dark. August had not moved.

When they reached Tallsman's car at the back of the building, Rogirsen placed the boy in the rear.

"Are you coming along?" Tallsman asked.

Rogirsen said, "No. You'll have to do it alone. I—" Then, shaking his head, he went away.

Tallsman started the car and drove slowly away from the school, watching the dark. Inside the main building, a single window shivered with light. Larkin's office. Tallsman passed the light but nobody came to chase him. He moved the car a little faster.

The clock on the dashboard read eleven forty-five. Reaching the road, Tallsman made the car leap forward.

He drove for home.

Third Day

CHAPTER 24

CHORUS:
Coming Near to the End of Time

Midnight had come again and gone and the island lay softly sleeping in its wake. Most of the people who lived here on the island were quiet people and had been well and fast asleep long before the coming of midnight, but here and there in isolated pockets, a few people, none like another, continued to move easily through the center of the night.

On the road between the school and the town, a car dashed through the mud and ruts. A man sat in the front seat of the car, holding the steering wheel tightly as if he were afraid that it might jump from his hands and assume a life and will of its own, but this was impossible, because the car was a bright new model and its directional equipment was firmly set and would never falter and the car possessed neither mind nor will of its own with which to assume a conscious existence. The man appeared to be unaware of these facts as his hands burned whitely, straining against the wheel.

The man was thinking: Oh no, now what? What can I do running me into the army at my advanced age with death an almost positive certainty and him lying naked and safe in the back secure in the back safe as a baby? Took control of my will among the trees and stream and Rogirsen all the rest of them the cabin where I saw it but not knowing truly what I saw. Oh no. Tin can empty container which once contained cold beans and the edge bright like a star and not a dash or taste of rust or rot. Must have been they. If so, where and Milinqua why August? Poor Corlin ought to forget and go back to where I love her like she loves me. This running fleeing skipping away in the dark toward the army not my responsibility and I've got children Stephanie all waiting for some kind of fast excuse. I can't fight— not me—too old—no human beings on the front. Instead, machines with glazed mechanical eyes and swords for fingers knives for toes.

In the rear of the car, a shape (not man, not boy, not being—a shape) lay hidden beneath the guise of sleep, but his lungs labored terrifically like those of a long distance runner. Inside its mind, all was dark and empty like an underground cavern. No movement. Not even a meditative thought or nonthought. The shape and the car—equally dark—glided together through the night, each firmly encased by its own emptiness. At the wheel, the man cried, deeply in thought.

Five minutes after twelve—and rolling.

Not far from the car's final destination stood the forty-one rising stories of the Pelly Tower. On the fourteenth floor in an isolated office, several men wandered aimlessly around a seated girl. The number of men in the office shifted constantly as one left carrying a thin strip of colored paper and another entered carrying a similar strip. The men avoided the girl as much as they could. They noticed that her eyes gleamed as brightly as day and this frightened them. Those men who were not afraid of her eyes were disgusted by her general condition, but this sense of disgust was actually a way of stifling their true fear, for these were men well accustomed to the necessity of hiding their real emotions.

Entering the office, a man passed a strip of colored paper to another man, who read the words printed upon it and nodded his head. This man thought: Making me sick poor girl destroyed by that thing wandering out there in the woods and they all know where but none will say. Milinqua half dead out there too by now probably having his mind eaten away like this poor girl and when he's dead everybody will finally rise a notch and won't it be awful because he wouldn't move up on his own. Still this girl makes me sick, looking at her.

The man dropped the paper on his desk and spoke aloud to the other men in the room. The girl was here in this room only temporarily and these men were glad of that. The thin strips of colored paper were messages from headquarters, the most recent of which confirmed that the girl would be taken down the island first thing in the morning and left with the men at the big research installation. There she would be observed and studied and tabulated. The men here knew she was somehow connected with this installation but none knew exactly how or why. And none cared. This was something outside their immediate range of vision. They could not concern themselves with it.

And the girl? She was thinking too: Water running uphill trees bursting like dogs in the wind trickling leaves and wandering men drying dying yes hello I've been waiting for you wetly to the inner ground's wet tube put this down oh cry and please don't please—

Ten minutes after twelve—and sighing.

Near by, a modest house lay darkly slumbering in the night, but in the living room of this house a woman was sitting. Around her the room was dark, and her face was lined and drawn and creased like an old road map. Her fingers wiped fitfully at her eyes and her cheeks were smeared with the lingering traces of vanished tears. This woman lived in this very nice house with its lovely garden and two delightful children. Right now she was quite alone. The garden lay far away outside and the children were sleeping. Her husband—he was gone.

Her thoughts came as tears, but these were new tears bearing no relation to the ones of despair which had flowed with the passing of the gray day. Her husband was gone, and now she was glad. She knew she had helped him to go, forced him to go, wanted him to go. She had wept before from the sorrow of separation, but now she knew how silly that had been. She was crying now, but for other and better reasons. Because she was happy. Because she was free. And because it was done.

A moment later, the woman got to her feet, wiping at her eyes. She thought she might like to smile, so she tried and the smile felt good, like a warm and happy mask. Keeping the smile, she left the room.

Fifteen minutes after twelve—and sleeping.

Near the school, the man stood encircled by the darkness of his home, peering deeply into the vague mists. This was such an ugly place, he saw, with clothes and garbage and rubbish tossed carelessly around the room. Had he really made his home here? And for so many years? For—wait—how many was it? He could not remember. Well, that part wasn't the important part. What difference were a few years?

Opening the door a crack, he peered outside. Now this was better. This was something clean and clear and correct. The voice was gone and he was alone. Now was his chance to use those senses which had gone untouched for so many years. It wasn't like before, when the voice had still been there. That had been like being a machine. He wasn't a machine now. He was a man, and it felt strange being a man this time; mostly it felt new and strange and different. He did not think he had ever been a man before. He could not recall it.

Looking at the night sky, he thought about his friends. He could remember his friends, but there had only been two. Tallsman and August, but soon he'd have more. He thought about Larkin, the man who had ridden his dreams like a demon. Poor Larkin, he thought. Then he thought about the woman—remembering her name—Corlin—and he felt sorry for her too. Poor Corlin, he thought. She was a lot like him, trapped by something beyond her control. He was free now. He sympathized with her. He wished her well.

Beyond the cottage, the night was a crystalline sculpture resting precariously atop the spinning planet. It felt good feeling sorry for someone else. So many years he had lived and during all that time he had never once felt sorry for someone besides himself. Now, transformed, reborn, whatever, he had found a whole new world, one so vast and wide and deep that it would take him a lifetime to determine its true size and shape. But he had lost something as well. He had lost the past. Those years were gone and only tiny bits and shreds remained, seconds and minutes rather than years. But what did he want with a past? What use could he make of those years? They were gone and done and wasted. He felt sorry for the rest of the human race, for all those billions of men and women destined to live their entire lives burdened by a constantly expanding past. The poor bastards, thought Michael Rogirsen.

Twenty minutes after twelve—and seeing.

In the north wing of the student dormitory of New Morning school, the children roamed sleeplessly through the darkened chamber. The two teachers watching tonight were the children's special favorites, since the two had far more in common with each other than with any of the children. So because of this, once the lights were out, neither teacher bothered to glance inside. Staying in their seats, they did whatever it was they liked to do together and left the children free to run and whisper and talk and cry.

Now, a few of them were asleep. A full hour had passed since the darkening of the lights, so a few were already talked out. But most of them were not. Many had hardly begun to talk, and these were the ones who skipped through the dark, darting from bunk to bunk, chattering like a flock of excited sparrows.

—They'll never catch him way down there in the woods. I don't think anybody even remembers that old cabin except Steven. He remembers everything. I'm sure they'll never find him till he's ready to be found.

—Shot him in the foot? Oh no, not really? Just like that? *Bang.* In the foot?

—We'd gone to town to deliver the message, see, and when we got back, there he was, all squatted down on the floor with his shoe off and a stream of blood thick as a river pouring out of his sock. I got sick. I thought Steven had blown his whole foot to hell, but he said no, it was only a scratch.

—He'll have to sign pretty soon and then it'll be over. I bet you he's done it by now or else Steven has blown his other foot off. In a way, you know, when it's over, I'll be sorry. It's really been fun.

Only two of the children in the room had actually participated in the day's events, but to hear them talk a person would think that each one of them had witnessed every single moment. Each seemed to know everything and wanted to tell it again and again to another, and this other also said he knew it all.

But there were a few who neither knew nor cared. A few who were left cold by the subject. These children also talked.

—Mother's coming up here to inspect the school.

—Oh no.

—Well, it's my fault, because I wrote her and said Larkin made us eat bugs for supper. She believed that, so I told her he was an old pervert who chased little girls. The younger, I said, the better. She believed that too.

—No.

—And I thought it was funny and would teach him a lesson. I showed him the letters but he just shrugged, so I went ahead and sent them. I was really mad at him. I had gone to see him and asked him why boys were shaped like they are and he told me it was because it made their pants fit.

—But you know why. You're eleven years old.

—Sure, but he still shouldn't have told me that. This'll teach him. Next time I bet he watches his mouth.

And there were others still who had reverted to a deeper, more meaningful world. For these children, a man's broken foot, a river of freshly flowing blood, an unsigned document, none of these things were more than mere insignificant trivia. These children were fully aware of the total nuances of real life. These children existed in the buried world of true dreams.

—I know I love him. What else can I say?

—But you can't love him. He's so old, almost seventeen if—

—But I do love him. That's the whole thing. When he touches me, looks at me, when he smiles, it's like—you wouldn't know—like falling off the highest mountain in the world and floating, flying, never reaching the ground. That's what he's like to me.

—But he doesn't love you. He can't.

—He does. I know he does. You wouldn't know.

—I know it's not love.

—And how would you know? Tell me that. Who would ever think of falling in love with you. You don't know the first thing about love, and that's the truth. Nobody would ever want somebody like you, so leave me alone. Please. Just leave me alone.

Twenty-five minutes after twelve—and passing.

The sparkling light in the ceiling painted the office with a yellow shimmering frost. The two men circled the woman like hunters stalking a deer. One hurled questions like bombs while the other, leaning back, spoke as softly as a contented cat. The old man, sitting behind the desk, clutched his heart as if it were a living and separate creature that demanded partial and individual love and care.

—You've got a family and you won't talk. I don't understand you. All I can think is that you don't give a damn for anybody but yourself—and this freak out there in the woods.

—But I don't know anything. How many times do I have to tell you? Why can't you believe me?

—Miss McGee. Please. I'm very sorry about this, but you must try to understand our position. We are aware of no logical reason for Dr. Larkin to be telling lies about you. Because of this, we have to assume that he's telling the truth. Now why don't you do the same? We aren't asking that you produce Mr. Milinqua. We merely ask that you divulge all the information that you have in your possession. Simply that.

—But I don't have any information.

—You want to find yourself on the front in a uniform? How about your father? He can't be a young man. Or your mother? How old is she? This isn't a joke. I think you ought to start talking. For their sake, for your own sake, for everyone's sake.

It was twelve-thirty when the office door opened from the outside.

Ford and Rutgers turned at the sound. Corlin heard, too, but she was too tired to move. She sat with her face buried in her hands.

—Mr. Milinqua!

—Yes, but what is happening here?

—Weren't you—?

—Yes? What?

—Weren't you kidnaped?

—What are you doing to this young lady?

—Questioning her, trying to find out—

—She knows nothing. Hasn't she told you?

—But he told us—

—I'm sure you misunderstood what he told you. Now I think both of you ought to go home. It's very late. Undoubtedly you are tired. Get a good night's sleep. I'll handle the investigation from this point.

—But how did you get loose?

—It wasn't difficult. They were children. Now—please—you must go.

—There's something wrong with your foot. Did—?

—It's nothing. I tripped in the woods. Now, please . . .

The two men went. Turning to Corlin, Milinqua smiled softly at her, and she smiled briefly back, then turned her eyes away.

Milinqua spoke to Larkin:

—I'm tired, too, Joyce. It has been a long day for all of us. I'll talk to you in the morning. Until then, good night.

Then he was gone, too. As quickly as that. And Larkin and Corlin were alone.

She looked at the door with an expression of dismay and relief. Shaking his head, Larkin removed his hand from his heart.

Corlin said:

—Why Joyce? Why?

It was thirty-five minutes after twelve.

And done.

CHAPTER 25

JOYCE LARKIN:
The Long Way Out

Corlin asked simply: "Why, Joyce? Why?"

She was standing across the desk from him, her arms dangling uselessly at her sides. He returned her stare and suddenly the office was too confining. The walls rushed straight at him like trains speeding toward a crossroads. He closed his eyes, the walls receded, and he rubbed his hands hopelessly across his chest.

"You won't tell me?"

"Is it necessary?" he asked. "Can't you see?"

"You're weak," she said.

"I'm broken."

"Why won't you tell me?"

"I'll tell you—but wait—give me time."

She nodded in agreement, her head jerking slowly as if the confirmation of a visible fact were in itself a painful experience. Larkin looked away from her. Then he said again, "Sit down, Corlin."

She sat down.

He said, "Think of me as a dead man. It's the easiest way. I am a dead man, don't you know? Dying separately in two distinct locations." He rapped his chest and patted his stomach. "Cancer down there eating at me right now as we sit here—and it's nothing new. It's been eating at me for ten years now. How old are you, Corlin? I've forgotten."

"Twenty-three," she said.

"I see," he said, forgetting the number immediately. What was a year but a series of days stacked one atop the other like slices of cut bread? Not many years; she was young. He kept that fact in mind while formulating his reply. He remembered that he too had once been young. And not so many years ago—less than seventy. He recalled those years in terms of shadowy fragments: fraternity parties packed with games and laughter; puttering automobiles that had to be shifted by hand; movie premières where even the spotlights seemed to shriek with glory; dinner parties that danced long past the first light of dawn. The people of his youth existed as dark figures mystically moving through these misty pageants. They were hardly real. Even his mother— even she was recalled merely as the leading player in an enormous, half-forgotten melodrama. But sometimes she had talked to him and he remembered that part clearly too.

"At the universities," he said. "Do you know if they still have fraternities?"

"How should I know? Joyce, please . . ."

She was impatient. But she was young. Looking at his hands, he glared at them as they rolled across his middle like lovers clinging to a rocking bed. He did not look at her this time.

"I'm sorry," he said. And he told her the details of his sickness.

"Then you're the one who told Milinqua." She laughed at him. Sorrow and pity dominated her laughter. But for him? he wondered. Or for herself. She said, "That's funny, because Tallsman thought it was Sheridan. He decided it had to be him because it couldn't be any of us, so he came and told me about it. I thought—I knew it had to be you. I knew it wasn't me and Clark's too stupid, and Tallsman too. Now at least I know why— that was the part I couldn't figure out—but now I don't know what changed your mind. Do you want to die now?"

"I don't know," he said. "But I didn't change my mind. Or did I? Milinqua and I are old friends. We understand each other. He is a very good man, a kind man. You wouldn't understand. You're too young, but when I was a boy, we called them gentlemen, and we pronounced the word as if it were two words.

Milinqua allows me the pleasure of doing things my own way. We spar like a couple of boxers—and then Steven came in and stayed—and how was I to know August would stand up and walk away? Eventually, in my own good time, I would have told him, and he knew that. I gave him some hints and he understood but August had already left. When he found him, he would have thanked me. He would have taken him away, and in return I would have received another year or two of life."

Corlin was laughing again, but the pity and sorrow had gone from her voice. He asked her to stop, but she would not.

"When you were searching for him," she said, words darting cleanly between her laughter. "Then you wanted to find him but you wanted to hand him over to Milinqua. Like Melissa."

"No," he said, waiting for her laughter to end, thinking as he waited how he had come to change his mind. How he had seen Melissa in the woods and fallen in love (not love—more than love—he had been in love many times and it wasn't like this), seeing the end result of all his years of striving, gazing upon Melissa and seeing it and hearing her sing, knowing this was what he had been trying to do ever since the day he had opened the school. Now, looking at Corlin, shivering as her laughter ended, he recalled that she was the most successful of all his children, that he had once felt that she was as near as he could come to producing that mythical creature, the healthy and whole human being. But take her and compare her with Melissa and see the difference—thinking this, he almost laughed aloud, but before he could begin, she had stopped. So he told her how he had come to change his mind.

"I cling to what's left of my life like a shipwrecked sailor hanging on to a shred of flotsam, knowing there's nothing near me but the sun alone in the sky and an unbroken sea of foaming water, but continuing to live in the hope that tomorrow will bring with it an excuse, a reason for living. And it has happened to me. I have my reason now. I have seen it."

"Rogirsen, too," she said.

"There will be others."

"Yes," she said. "But why didn't you tell those men? Why did you tell them I knew about the kidnaping? You knew I didn't."

He smiled and told her. He had known he was a weak man. Those two men had frightened him. The older a man, the weaker he was. That didn't seem fair, but at least he knew how to control his weaknesses. Corlin was young and strong and she had withstood their questioning in a fashion he never could have managed. And, too, he had guessed that Milinqua would soon be coming. Milinqua was another man not apt to be hampered by his own weak points.

She said she understood.

"How late is it?" he asked.

"I think it must be close to two o'clock."

"Then will you help me?" Standing, he discovered that his knees were weak. He tried to cross the room and she caught his elbow and guided him to the door. "I'm tired," he told her. "That's all."

She said she understood and they went outside.

Beneath them, the creek flowed darkly, running through the night. They stood on the rickety wooden bridge, which Larkin himself had constructed years ago, and looked down at the water below. Larkin held himself braced against the railing, and the tired wood rustled in the wind. Laying a hand on top of his, Corlin pressed down.

"It's a dark night tonight," he said. "I had almost forgotten that it was here. We've been inside a long time." He had regained a measure of his strength and had walked this far without help. But now he wanted to pause and rest before completing the journey. He looked down at the water and it made him dizzy, the narrow black knife of the stream cutting deeply through the night. Out there beyond, August was waiting. And Rogirsen now—she had told him about Rogirsen. He was glad about that. Another man had been set free.

Corlin said, "When I was a girl, I was in love with you. Have I ever told you that?"

He said, "No," trying to keep his voice free of irritation. But he did not feel like talking now. Or listening. What he wanted to do was watch the water flowing below and think quiet thoughts to himself, gliding darkly along within the river of his own mind. But Corlin's voice was insistent; she said no. And at last he relented and removed himself from the multiple complexities of thought. He listened to her.

She said, "I thought you were the greatest of them all. I had read the others—starting when I was twelve with Freud—and I knew what they had done, all of them, and how important it had been, but as far as I was concerned you were the one who had taken all their jumbled theories and contradictory thoughts and made them into a practical workable whole, and I knew I was the end result of all that work, the final recipient of your knowledge and wisdom, and I guess that's why it was hard for me to avoid falling in love with you." Her hand pressed tightly against his, as snug as two interlocking pieces of a jigsaw puzzle. "And my love for you was even greater than that, I think, because I was sure all along that there had to be more. I knew what I was, you see, and I couldn't believe that was all. I was sure you had even more things to give me but I knew you wouldn't give them unless I proved to you that I was truly deserving of them. So that's why I tried so hard. That's why I learned how to conduct the therapy sessions and took over your work and left you free to do whatever you wanted to do. I can remember that I felt the same way about my father, wanting to do everything that he ever did. But I didn't want it to be like that with you. I knew that wouldn't be right, so I kept trying harder and harder till finally I got too tired to try any more and I gave up. That's when I stopped. I couldn't go any further."

Larkin said he thought he understood. He had listened to her and he knew she had been speaking honestly. But he really understood her no more than he understood the water that ran below, blacker than the night which circled it. Or the stars winking blinking above, hidden by distant looming clouds, and there was the moon way up on high, and the wind whistling, brushing his hands and face. Larkin chewed his lip. It was cold. He shivered.

He was sitting on the edge of the bed, looking up at her. She had not finished yet, she was still talking, but he sensed that she was approaching the end.

She said, "So I brought him here and we looked at your bed and I thought to draw him down like we had intended. But I didn't. I couldn't. The other time, the first time, in the cottage, it had been all right that time, but looking at your bed, wanting to come even closer to you, I knew it wouldn't be right, I couldn't do it, so I took him away and we found this room here and this same bed. It was awful. You know that. Long before the end, he went mad, screaming and shouting, lashing at my skin and my eyes. He had been as near to you as I could ever come without actually having you. But he was too far away. Then he was gone. Do you understand me?"

"I think I do," Larkin said. "But, Corlin—think—I'm too old now." Her hips stood evenly on a level with his eyes. Her hands nervously toyed with the flaps of her blouse and skirt. Beyond, the night crept fearlessly through an unshaded window and doused the room faintly with darkness.

He had tried to explain, but she shook her head. "But no please just say you will yes please."

"Don't beg me," he said.

"Say yes."

"All right," he said. "All right—yes," and he held out his arms. He could not have said anything else, old as he was, too old for saying no. She came hurriedly against him, afraid to wait, and he thought he might be able to do it properly if he could only find the right way through the familiar patterns of the past. He tried that way, going back, drawing the past close around him. Mother saying you're better than any and she warning him about the girl from whose father was and not the first time owner of a chain of discount stores from coast to coast.

"Corlin," he said softly, dropping the past, forgetting the past. He removed her blouse and let it slip to the floor. The past would not help him. He laid a tentative hand on her breast. The smooth flesh of her youth was a tiny hill beneath the hard grim flesh of his palm. He tried to forget about that too. He pressed harder and rubbed the whirling ridges of her nipple. He dipped toward the abrupt warmth of her middle. He was trying. Lowering herself, she rolled between him. They kissed.

"Joyce," she said.

And that was the last either of them said.

He performed like a gentleman, moving easily and slowly, as tender as a father, coming close and not surprised when he discovered that he was ready. That meant nothing. That meant the past was gone, but he had already known that. She was his now, and he held her gingerly as if she were a child. He was not shamed by the nearness of death. He listened to her, knew her reality, if not for him, then for whomever she thought he was.

And he pressed his lips deep into the flesh of her shoulder.

When it came, it came slowly. It acted as if it had never expected to be called again, as if it had slept and was now slowly waking, but coming, for him and her, coming for both.

Afterward, he held her tightly in his arms, for he had learned half a century ago that this was the essential moment for a woman. To her, lying here, sex had merely been a prelude to love. He nestled close to her. The darkness came down and covered them both like a shroud. He sighed and let it surround them.

Later, she said, "I thought I was in love with Tallsman. Can you imagine that? But it was only because of you and—I trusted him! And I still do. But now I have you to trust."

"Don't."

"Why not?"

"Just don't," he said. "I'm going to die soon."

"Oh, don't talk about that now," she said. "I don't want to talk about anything right now. All my life it's been talk and talk. I want to stop for a minute. Do you understand?"

"I think I do," he said.

When she was ready to leave, he asked her to switch on the light and do him a favor and stand naked and turn on her heels so that he could see all of her. She was happy to do as he asked, smiling as she did it, and he watched her turn, slowly once, then twice. He closed his eyes and told her it was all right to go.

When she had gone, behind closed eyelids, he watched as she continued to turn, whirling around and around, again and again.

He knew he could die willingly now. He had an image fine enough to carry with him to the grave. Waiting, he called upon death and asked it to come. His eyes remained tightly sealed.

But death did not come. Sleep came. Waiting beyond the window, death may have watched him. But it did not come. If anything, death had been amused by him. Death was never that easy.

CHAPTER 26

CORLIN MC GEE:
Automatic Rundown

Corlin fastened the totality of her attention onto the road, her hands gripping the dashboard controls that served to disconnect the automatic system of the car and allow the driver to guide the vehicle manually around and beyond unforeseen obstacles. She knew this was hardly necessary right now in spite of the poor condition of the road caused by yesterday's continual rain and normally she would have curled up in the back and rested until the car delivered her home, but she felt she had to do something now. She couldn't rest. She was tensed up tighter than a drum, zooming higher than a kite, and there was no other available outlet where she could rid herself of this excess energy, nothing but the winding road ahead of her, no place left to run, so what else was she supposed to do now? That was the part they had never explained to her. Where was she supposed to go now that it was done? Home? With Sheridan? To sleep? It was already close to morning, and each passing minute seemed to make her more fully awake than the last. How could she ever get to sleep? She was beginning to think she would never be able to sleep another wink—she was almost sure of that. Oops —a mudhole. She guided the car neatly around it and felt as proud as a child completing his first successful bicycle ride.

Poor Corlin McGee, thought Corlin McGee. What can she do with this crazy furious churning mixed-up life they've given her? And now Larkin. And of course, that had not been nearly the way she had expected. But what ever was? Not that Joyce hadn't been a tender lover—he was that and a gentleman too—but now that it was over and done, what was she supposed to do? Was it always going to be this way, her whole life, achieving what she had always desired and then discovering that it wasn't what she had really wanted after all? Well then, what was it she wanted now? Wasn't that the whole problem? Because she did not know. There didn't seem to be anything left. For the first time, she moved through life toward a blank future. There was nothing which said, *This is what you're going to do next, Corlin.* Her last goal had been achieved; Joyce was her lover. But now, so what? So it had been a comforting hour or two, good but not great, and although he had tried to understand, it had not worked, not completely, so now what?

Her headlights caught them neatly, drawing the four figures out of the shadows and placing them evenly in the forefront of her vision. As soon as she saw what they were, she stopped the car. They were standing near the edge of the road at the end of a long curve where any passing motorist would be sure to see them. She hadn't recognized them—but they were children—and they were here. She heard them coming toward the car as she sat in the dark. Their feet pattered and squished through the wet and mud. She waited.

A finger tapped her window. Sliding across the seat, she touched a lever which unleashed a circle of light that surrounded the car. Then she lowered the window. Only one child had come, and he was leaning against the car. He smiled at her. She thought she saw the other three waiting beyond the edge of the light.

"Hello, Steven," she said, calmly.

"Aren't you surprised to see me?"

"I don't think anything could surprise me now. What are you doing out here?"

"Waiting for you," he said.

"I should have known. Who's with you?"

"Just some of the kids. I've got a message for you. From August."

That didn't surprise her either. "Is that why you let Milinqua go?" she asked.

"That's right."

"Where is he? August?"

"He went home with Tallsman. That's the message. He wants to see you."

"In Tallsman's house?"

Steven thought that was funny. "No," he said. "In the back yard. There's a house there built in a tree. That's where they're hiding. He's got something he wants you to do for him."

"And you don't know what?" she said.

"Not me. He wants you right away."

"I'll go now," she said. She was staring at the boy. What she saw surprised her. He had been changed, all right; that much she could plainly see. But the changes were not nearly so obvious as Melissa's. Steven seemed to stand taller in his shoes. His eyes were clear and his face was confident. Small changes such as these—but many of them.

"Are you all right?" she asked him.

"Sure. Why shouldn't I be?"

"No reason," she said. And that was right: there was really no reason to expect enlightenment to affect everyone the same way.

"I've got to go now," he said. "I'll see you later." He stepped away from the car, waving at her. He was gone into the darkness. She heard the others moving away with him.

And now four, she thought, remembering Melissa and Rogirsen. That meant there were six of them now. The car was moving, she suddenly realized, and she couldn't remember starting it. She didn't care. She set the directional equipment to take her home, then turned off the interior light and leaned back and rested, not sleeping, her eyes kept open. At least she had somewhere to go now, she told herself; at least that was a beginning.

Obediently, the car halted in front of her home. She decided that she needed a few moments of additional rest, so she sat quietly in the car and stared at the apartment building in front of her. It stretched eight stories into the sky, a wide dark concrete box. There were a hundred and ten units in the complex, she remembered. Of these, fifty-five were one-room studios (most equipped with a kitchen the approximate size and shape of a large cupboard); the remaining fifty-five apartments were one-bedroom units such as the one she and Sheridan occupied. How many people actually lived in this building? she wondered. Two hundred—oh, more than that, she was sure—three hundred at least, or three hundred and fifty. And why? The island was rich with vacant land. There was more than enough room so that everyone could have his own home with an acre of bare land separating him from his nearest neighbor. So why did everyone want to live in a place like this? Or the other one two blocks down the street, or the one after that, all of them just the same, equally as big and impersonal, just as dark. It sometimes seemed to her as if the whole human race were trying with all its enormous might to squeeze itself into a single vast room. And what would things be like in a hundred years? She took a glance ahead at the year 2104 and discovered eight billion human beings living in a single enormous building while the remainder of the living earth, green and blue and golden, ran wildly free around it.

She drew her thoughts back from the future and turned the car, letting it glide through the night. It ran down streets, shifting and turning and rumbling, and she watched the passing buildings and it seemed as if each ran flowing into the next, ignoring space and time, running like quick white water. At last there was only one building and she realized it was Tallsman's house. She had arrived.

Getting out of the car, she approached the house, but she did not try to go inside. Instead, she went around to the back yard, where the grass was shining with yellow light as dawn peeped above the horizon. She saw a tree, a big towering weather-beaten madroña, near the center of the yard and went toward it. She wasn't surprised to discover a homemade rope ladder hanging from a low branch. She climbed the ladder easily and, reaching the top, pulled herself inside the tree house. It was badly constructed and unpainted and looked as though a moderate wind would send it spinning toward the ground. Some boards overlapped others and there were huge holes and gaps in the walls and ceiling. It was dark inside the tree house but she could see.

She said, "August," speaking softly, almost whispering.

He did not reply, but she knew he was there and sensed he was awake.

Moving silently, she crawled around Tallman's slumbering form, glancing briefly at the man she had once loved, and went to August's side. The boy was awake. His eyes were open but his face was cold and expressionless. This was the first time she had seen him since that first night and she was surprised that he looked the same as he always had.

She whispered his name again.

There was a voice in her mind: *So you've come.*

"Yes," she whispered. His voice did not frighten her. "I met Steven on the road."

We'll wait here till morning. You'll need to rest.

"I'm not tired. Is there—?"

Yes. But it's too soon now. Why not rest for a few hours?

"What is it you want me to do?"

Later, said the voice.

"You don't want to tell me?"

The voice did not answer her this time. She looked at August and squinted and saw that his eyes were staring coldly at her. But he was smiling. In his smile, she saw a way out of these endless complications one piled on top of another until it was impossible to see the light, and the buildings that ran and flowed, and all these people she could never understand—people like Tallsman and Sheridan and Larkin—how was she supposed to know which one she really wanted?

She asked August to help her.

Not now. Now I need your help. Perhaps later.

She wanted to argue with him. But she guessed that it was useless. Turning over, she lay flat on the floor and stared at the roof. She was tired but she did not want to sleep. She waited for the end of dawn, but it was slow in coming.

CHAPTER 27

GREGORY TALLSMAN:
Morning Dew

Tallsman was awake now. He wanted to open his eyes and smile and greet yet another day, but he couldn't. Before he could open his eyes, he had to regain control of his body. Who controlled it now? He wasn't sure of that, but he knew it was someone besides himself. Sometime during the night, he had been forced to relinquish control of his own body, and something else had moved in and taken the reins. He sensed that this something else had gone now. If it hadn't, he would not have been awake. The way was wide open for him to regain possession of what was rightfully his. But he had to find the way. So he tried.

He tried, and felt himself moving a little bit closer, felt his body lying as near to him as a loyal wife to a good husband, but he couldn't seem to bridge those last few inches. He tried not to panic. He knew he had to keep calm. He thought that maybe if he managed to reconstruct the events that had led to this loss, then perhaps he could find a way of rediscovering his body. He tried this, but the past was beyond him and he could not find it either. So he tried another way. He tried to remember how it was to see and smell and hear and feel. He stretched his senses—and was that an odor? *No*—but wasn't that the feel of cool air rustling his skin and hair? *No*—but wasn't that the hum of a passing airplane? Or—*yes*—the smell of bacon popping in an open skillet.

Struggling and straining, Tallsman all at once found that his eyes were open.

There was a flat expanse of cracked knotted wood lying directly above him. Here and there, a rusty bent nail protruded from the wood, and there were wide gaps where flashes of blue and white gleamed like water.

Then a voice penetrated: "So you've decided to wake up."

Turning his head, Tallsman focused on the object beside him. It took a moment, but he recognized her. "Corlin," he said. "I was having a dream where I'd lost control of my body. Something else was running me."

"I hope you got it back," she said.

"I think so." He noticed himself wiping sleep from his eyes. Angrily, he dropped his hands and turned to study his surroundings. There was more wood and more nails, much cool morning air, and another object. He spoke to this object: "August."

August said, "Good morning, Mr. Tallsman," in a crisp boyish voice.

Tallsman turned back to Corlin and regarded her closely. There was something about her and another place. Another time. Yes, it was yesterday. For a moment, he saw it clearly, then yesterday seemed to slide away from him till it was as far away as last year. He asked her what she was doing here.

"August sent for me. He has something he wants me to do."

"What's that?"

"Nothing."

He had his senses and body under strict control now. He managed to clear a large part of the fog from his memory. He knew they were sitting on the floor of his children's tree house, which meant they were in the yard behind his house. He remembered about August and Milinqua and Rogirsen and all of last night.

"He wants you to do something for him, too," Corlin said.

Tallsman spoke to August: "You were asleep last night, or unconscious, when I brought you here. Do you remember what happened?"

"Yes," August said.

"Well, I don't. What happened at the cabin?"

"They let him go," Corlin said. "He came to Larkin's office and made them release us. August changed the children. I saw them."

"Steven?" Tallsman asked.

"Yes. That's what August wants you to do for him. He wants you to drive him to the children. They've got Melissa but the others are waiting at the cabin."

"That's not a very safe place."

"August says it is."

"He ought to know," Tallsman said. "But where are you going to be?"

"I have to go into town."

He shrugged and crawled away from her. "We might as well get going," he said, sticking his head into the light of day and glancing downward at the earth. The morning breeze moved evenly around him, carrying the promise of a clean day. Above, the sun was bright and rising in the sky. The madroña leaves turned fitfully in the air.

Climbing carefully down the ladder, Tallsman stretched his tired muscles. After a moment, August came after him. They reached the ground and crossed the yard together. As they passed the house, Tallsman listened and he thought he heard Stephanie and the children moving inside. He did not know what time it was but he guessed it was early yet. His family had only recently emerged from their beds. Stephanie would be cooking breakfast in the kitchen and preparing the children for school, and if he had been there, he would have been at the kitchen table, watching her cook, maybe eating already or sipping a cup of coffee, or maybe just doing nothing, sitting and thinking about the coming day. In ten or fifteen minutes, he and the children would leave the house. He would climb in the car and turn it toward the school and drive away while the children would stand at the corner and wait for the bus to come and take them to school. That would make it nine o'clock. He thought about Stephanie alone now in the empty house. Was she thinking about him? Did she know he was here? Had she seen the car parked in front of the house and wondered about it? He hadn't seen her in a day or more and they hadn't talked since that night when he had offered her a final chance and she had refused to take advantage of it. He hadn't even been able to think much of her lately. There had been too many other things on his mind, and she had long ago ceased to play an essential role in his life. But she was his wife. He had to keep reminding himself of that. So what if Corlin were his lover, and so what if yesterday afternoon had been better than all the many afternoons which had preceded it, those with Stephanie, even those he had spent with his first wife? Perhaps he could ask August to help Stephanie. Wasn't that why he was here? If so, what was he doing running around helping children by turning them into enlightened gods, boys ten years old and girls who were thirteen and fourteen? Why couldn't he help some of the millions of adult, full-grown men and women in the world who really needed a breath of life blown into their sagging souls? Like Stephanie. Or himself. Or Rogirsen. Now that had been the right way of using his powers. But why Melissa and the other children? He almost stoppped and asked August why, pointing to the house, but he did not. They were already sitting in the car and it was time to go.

Tallsman set the directional equipment for the school and the car slipped away from the house. Turning, he took a last look at his home and thought he glimpsed a flash of pale white crossing the window. But he wasn't sure.

He said, "I think my wife saw us. She might do something. She thinks you're a spy."

"No, that's all right," said August.

Tallsman nodded. He should have known better. Of course it was all right—well then, fine. If he had been August, it would have been all right with him too. But would he want to be August? He glanced at his companion as the car swerved onto the road which led to the school, tires slicing through ankle-deep mud and spraying water high against the windshield. Tallsman knew that he had never been able to understand August. Even before, when August had been just another twelve-year-old lower student, his origins somewhat clouded by a faint hint of mystery, even then he had never seemed to possess more than a bare functional rudimentary surface personality. Now, supposedly changed and transformed, reborn into a state of true enlightenment, a legitimate figure of cosmic mystery, he was even more of a cypher than before. He was not at all like either Melissa or Rogirsen. There was no aura of wisdom and maturity about him, no clinging halo of glimmering awareness. He acted as one would expect a twelve-year-old boy to act. There didn't seem to be anything about him which one could firmly grasp hold of, except a handful of interchangeable facial expressions, a nod and a shake and an occasional smile, a deepening frown, a voice heavily tinged by adolescence, a vocabulary that was colorless and bare. Tallsman had always liked August, but he had never come near to feeling that he understood him. No—wait—that wasn't right. He saw that now. He had understood August, and he did now, and that was the problem, for he had to assume that there was more to the boy than what he could see, that no one of August's age could be as limited and empty as this boy seemed. For someone so young, August was almost totally lacking in individual personality distinctions. He blended with the general mass of students, and this was surprising, because nearly all children are truly and distinctly individual; it's only when they grow older and approach the brink of adulthood that they begin to take upon themselves the accepted personality characteristics of those around them, only then that they willingly faded into the mass of common humanity. Some didn't, of course. But only a few. Larkin, for one, never had, but Tallsman could not think of any others he personally knew.

August told Tallsman to stop the car. Tallsman stopped the car and then August told him to move it off the road and park it behind a stand of trees, where it would not be visible from the road. Tallsman complied and then they walked into the woods, moving down what appeared to be an abandoned dirt road, one not used in many years since it was so badly overgrown with weeds and bushes that it blended naturally with the surrounding terrain.

"The cabin's at the end of this road," said August.

Tallsman nodded and walked along. He wanted to ask August if he could explain some of the things he had been thinking about, but he was hesitant to ask. For one thing it sounded so absurd: Can you explain to me why you don't happen to have a personality? Most people do, you know. Why not you, August? Don't you need to be a person? And for another, he was afraid that August might not be able to explain. He might not know —or worse yet, he would explain, but the explanation would be something Tallsman preferred not to hear. He made an effort to force all these unpleasant thoughts into some dark and secluded corner of his mind. He tried instead to concentrate on something else, something better. Like Corlin. He plucked a past image of her from his memory and studied it carefully. It was an image that should have excited him. At the very least, it should have pleased him. But it did neither. It was a clear and firm image too, but that was wrong as well, for Tallsman knew that when he really wanted to think of an image it was almost impossible to do so, that the image kept shifting and blurring and becoming something or someone else, something different. It was only when he did not really care that he could evoke a mental image as clear as this one, as unblurred as a fine photograph. He let Corlin go. He told her to go back to from where she had come, and concentrated instead on the road. They came to the creek and it was narrow here and they both jumped it and continued onward. Tallsman started to tell August about last night, about how he and Rogirsen had followed the creek through the night and seen the trees like sentinels standing above and then leaning down and blocking the moon and stars, but August said no, he knew all about it, and Tallsman returned his attention to the road.

They came to the cabin. In the light of day, it appeared more ravaged and beaten than last night. Tallsman could see grass growing tall on the broken roof, and there was no longer a feeling of mystery about the place. That too had gone with the night. Here was an old cabin, where a series of old men had once lived, and now that the men were gone and dead, the cabin was going with them. Tallsman heard voices coming from inside and he guessed that the children were there. He waited outside, obediently, while August passed inside. He sat in the wet grass that circled the cabin like a collar of green and plucked a moist blade from the ground and put it between his lips. He chewed the grass. It tasted sweet and moist and cool.

He tried to listen to the children, but they had fallen silent as soon as August entered the cabin or else they were whispering very softly. Something was up, Tallsman knew, but he also knew that he really did not give a damn. It was as if he had reached the end of a long and treacherous road only to discover that the road had run a circle and that he had returned to his point of departure. Now the others were eager to begin the journey again, but not him. He was content to stay where he was, sitting on the ground, chewing the grass. He thought it was a good life for him.

Time continued to pass and Tallsman continued to think, but finally August came out of the cabin. The children followed him. There were four of them, two girls and two boys, and Tallsman knew them all. He said hello to each in turn. August said, "We're going to the school now."

"Is that safe?" Tallsman asked.

"We have to go," one of the girls answered. Her name was Lorcas. She was a pretty girl. Thirteen, maybe fourteen, but still a lower. She was the kind of pretty girl who would make a beautiful woman. Her eyes were big and bright like two blue moons. She smiled at him and added, "August says so."

"All right," said Tallsman, speaking only because he wanted an extra moment in which to study the girl. She had changed, he decided. It was definitely there. Her eyes were bigger than ever, he decided, but now they sparkled with a sense of maturity that had never been there before, and her voice and stance and posture were those of a woman, not a young girl.

Before he had a chance to look at the others, they began to move away from the cabin. He hurried and fell into line, walking at the rear behind Lorcas. He watched her walking, her hips shifting easily beneath her thin white summer dress, her shoulders riding high and taut against the fabric of the garment, and her hair brushing against her bare arms, twitched and twirled by the wind. Taking two quick steps, he drew even with her, then walked at her side.

"Are you happy now?" he asked her.

"Yes," she said.

CHAPTER 28

MICHAEL ROGIRSEN:
Broken Sanctuary

"I don't understand," he said.

"You will, you will," cried Larkin, his hands becoming fists which pounded his desk, then as mere hands returning again to his chest. "I have to tell someone, and you're here. No one else is here, so please, please listen to me, remember what I tell you, and when I'm gone, consider it, think of what I've said, and maybe you will be able to understand. Someone must know before I'm gone and I can't wait any longer to talk."

"Yes, all right," said Rogirsen, who did not understand. Not yet.

Sunlight sliced through the open window, spilling across the room in a flickering but even line and painting Larkin's face with orange and yellow when it reached him, but he appeared not to notice the light. His hands were held firmly across his chest, and his chair was shoved back from the desk. The top of the desk was bare, with two glaring exceptions. The first of these exceptions was a sheet of white typewriter paper, the clean surface of which was marred by a series of large handwritten scrawls. Leaning forward from where he sat, Rogirsen tried to read these scrawls but he could not quite fix them in his eye. But he knew what they meant. He did not have to read them to know what they meant. What they meant was:

> Taking my own life because this way is the only way to ensure continued existence for those who deserve it far

more than me. Eighty-year-old man here writing and the last ten of these years have been lived while dead and now I want to go to the grave where all dead men ought to lie. I have a reason for wanting to go now, and I have never had such a good reason before. It's easier this way than waiting for the slow consuming teeth down inside me to come clawing up to end it the slow, painful way. Maybe this means I'm a coward but there's no way for me to know this for sure. I suppose I'll never be able to know. Since I'll be dead.

The note had not been signed. The second exception was a gun. Rogirsen knew next to nothing about guns, but this one looked big and bright and dark and shiny. It was black.

"Listen to me," cried Larkin.

"I'm listening," Rogirsen said. He lifted a hand and shaded his eyes, though the sun stood at his back and his eyes were already firmly encased within the shadows. He performed this gesture for Larkin's benefit, but the old man did not appear to notice or care. Rogirsen said, "May I turn off the light? It's very bright in here now."

"Yes yes of course—but, Michael, please listen. I must hurry."

Rogirsen went and switched off the overhead electric light. The room darkened imperceptively, and he returned and stood across from Larkin, watching the old man's quivering hands trembling against his tossing lungs. Rogirsen sought to glimpse this man as something less than evil, struggled to discern the humanity which surely lay inside him, wanting to make him into something more real and definite than a private and personal devil. Who was this man as a man except a tired old man who talked about the inconsequential aspects of suicide? Was this man the same man who had ridden his life like a winged demon for so many years? It hardly seemed possible. But I've changed too, Rogirsen thought.

But he did not know. He knew he had a headache and he wished he had been able to sleep last night. Of course if he could have slept, he would have slept and been sleeping now. He would not be here. At dawn he had seen the light shining and had come, surprised by his own need for human contact. He had found Larkin. Exactly like this.

"Are you through now, Michael? Are you going to listen to me now? You can't make me stop. Not this way. So stop trying and just listen. I have to get these things out of my system and I know you don't mind."

"I don't mind," confirmed Rogirsen. "I'll listen."

"Good, good, fine, fine. Then listen. It began the day they bought my soul—am I being dramatic?—and that happened years ago when I first began to feel the pains in my stomach. I guessed what it had to mean and I went to them and they told me yes. And they said if you live out your life and keep in step, never trying anything new, then we'll provide you with a life to live. Do you understand?"

"Yes," said Rogirsen, who truly understood. Not from Larkin's jambling phrases, inarticulate as they were, but from the pictures which accompanied those words, the visions that churned and snapped behind his eyes. These visions were not something new. Rogirsen had been seeing them as long as he could remember. People talked and he saw what they were talking about. But always before the pictures had been faint and blurred and not even there unless he concentrated upon them to the exclusion of all else, including the conversation itself, and if he concentrated upon the pictures and lost the conversation, then he saw the pictures but he did not know what they meant, so he usually ignored them, acted as if they were not really there, but this time they were clear and for a moment they frightened him, the fierce colorful intensity of these visions, but then he was not afraid any longer, because the pictures grabbed him and swept him up and forced him to watch and listen. The pictures were too powerful to permit fear.

Larkin said, "Good, then listen." He said, "All of this is only a prelude to the true events that began the day they came to me and said we have created this creature in our laboratories the same way we created those perfect soldiers who now do our fighting for us, but this one is different and we don't quite know what to make of him because we don't think he's achieved full maturity yet, so what we want you to do, Larkin, is take him in and let him live here at your school and see how he reacts in a normal but controlled environment. Mr. Milinqua, the local area supervisor, is aware of all this, and as soon as anything untoward happens with our creature, we want you to report the fact to Mr. Milinqua immediately. The creature will have the surface appearance and knowledge and attitudes of a common nine-year-old boy, and I agreed, of course, since I'd been agreeing with them for years and didn't know what else to do, having the habit of saying yes without thinking, and they fixed it up so that Tallsman and I stumbled upon the boy one day and took him in. For several years, nothing happened. And then it did that night when it finally did happen, and I made my report and Milinqua came rushing out to investigate. We sparred and Steven came into the room and I tossed him some hints and August went and disappeared, but then I discovered exactly what they had given me, when we found Melissa I saw it, and I knew that August was not some special breed of monster but instead what he was was the end result of all my years of teaching, and then I couldn't turn him in. It would have meant turning myself in, the same thing, my whole life. Nor was I sure about anything by this time. I thought: Why is this boy the way he is? Did they plan it this way? Is it because of their tampering with him in the laboratory, cutting genes and splicing molecules, or is it because of what we have done to him here, Corlin and I, pushing him back and opening his lives so that, seeing, he has become what he now is? And they had never told me anything about him. And I had never dared ask. They had never said this creature is one who can merge with other normal human beings the way certain lower animals can merge with others of their kind. They never told me that, never explained anything, and maybe they didn't know either. Maybe that means I'm right and it was me and it was Corlin. Maybe it was Intensive Therapy. I think they thought they had created another of their human weapons, like the soldiers, a machine made out of flesh and blood without either feeling or soul. Now he's free. They won't want me now. I've turned on them by turning back to what I've always believed. That leaves me with only one way out."

Rogirsen said, "Yes, I understand."

"You do?" Larkin reached down and patted the gun. Lifting it, he turned it slowly in his hands as if it were a toy.

"Not that," Rogirsen said. "I mean I understand about August."

"You do? Well, I suppose you should. He's helped you, hasn't he?"

"Yes," Rogirsen said. "He has helped me. And I was thinking. Perhaps he can help you too."

"Don't say that," said Larkin.

"Why not?" Rogirsen shrugged. "You don't want to die, do you?"

"I don't want to die."

"Then don't hurry your way into it. Wait for August. What can it hurt?"

"Nothing," said Larkin. He dropped the gun and it clattered noisily against the desk. "I think I've been acting like a fool."

"Probably," Rogirsen said.

Larkin lowered his head and caught it with his hands. "Do you really think he can help me? Are you just saying that to make me stop? Don't be afraid to tell me the truth." He jerked his head at the gun. "I won't use it."

"He helped me. I don't see why he can't help you."

"It's different."

"Not really. I was suffering from a disease the same as you. Mine was a disease of the mind and yours is a disease of the body. That's the only difference."

"I'll ask him," Larkin said. "I'm ready for him now. I need some peace. Everything has—"

"I'm not peaceful," Rogirsen said. "Or enlightened. I'm normal. And I had to get that way by myself. August didn't save me. He just let me glimpse the world outside myself for a few hours. After that, it was up to me."

Larkin was laughing. "This is funny. You saving my life when for years you would have killed me if I'd allowed you half an opportunity."

"I said I was normal now."

"So I see."

"And I feel I owe you something."

"How?"

"Because you let me live here. I was dangerous, especially to you, and you let me stay. You could have had me locked up."

"You were my failure. Corlin was my success. Or so I thought. I let both of you stay."

"I owe you something for that."

"Perhaps you do. I can't say. But at least I've told my story now, and that's something. Wait and wait, I suppose. What else can we do except that? Wait and see what happens tomorrow —isn't that the way it has to be?—and if I'm going to die, then I suppose I'll just go ahead and do it. For a while there, I thought I had a reason for going now. But all I was was tired, very tired."

"I came here to tell you that I'd forgiven you. I suppose I can say that now."

"Thank you," Larkin said.

"And I wanted to ask if you could forgive me."

"I could, yes. But I don't have anything to forgive you for. I really wish I did."

"Thank you," Rogirsen said. Getting to his feet, he crossed the room and looked out the window straight at the sun. He watched the brightness of morning light and saw, distantly, trees waving happily in the breeze, and near by was the faint blue slash of the creek, and near that stood the strong flat roof of his cottage. Rogirsen knew he would be leaving here soon. Maybe he ought to go today—go right now. This wasn't his home any longer. He had finally graduated. It was time to take a look at the rest of the world.

"I don't even have any idea what it's like out there," he said, facing the window. "What's happened to the rest of the world while I've been locked up here, living in a nightmare?"

"Nothing you would have wanted to have seen."

"Maybe not," Rogirsen said. "There's somebody coming." He put his nose against the glass and watched the straggling figures coming slowly toward the school. Their outlines wavered uncertainly, shifting like mirages beneath the heavy light. But he knew they were real and he knew who they were. He turned to tell Larkin.

"It's Corlin," he said. "And Milinqua. And two other men. I suppose they're looking for August. I suppose it's not over yet."

"I didn't think it was," Larkin said. "Corlin, you say?"

"Yes, she's with them."

"You had better go yourself, Michael. They'll want you if they know you're here."

"Yes, you're right," Rogirsen said. He went to the door. "Good-by," he said.

"Come back if you can," Larkin said.

"I'll try." He left, not looking back, and moved down the corridor toward the outside. Passing closed doors, he heard the hum of voices from behind them and realized it was much later than he had thought. There was an open door and he paused a moment and glanced through. The class was proceeding well. A teacher stood beside the blackboard, where strange white scrawls nibbled at the edges of wisdom, and a student said, ". . . but that's the part I don't understand." Then the teacher was explaining that part, and Rogirsen knew it was time to go. He went away, resuming his previous course. His footsteps echoed, ricocheting off the walls and ceiling. Tossing open a door, he fled. He dashed ahead into the lighted world of the sun.

CHAPTER 29

CORLIN MC GEE:
Realm of Magic

"I believe we're going to have a fine day today," said Milinqua, as they crossed the grounds.

"Yes," Corlin agreed, glancing briefly at the bright cloudless sky above and continuing to walk as quickly as possible, trying to keep pace with this man who walked as though walking were an exercise requiring no more effort than sleeping. But Corlin did not want to walk this quickly. She would rather have dropped to her knees and crawled toward the school, for she was no longer as certain as she had been a moment before that this course was the right one to follow. But he had told her that he wanted it done, and when he had said it, she had not seen anything wrong with his thinking, but now she was beginning to wonder.

"I hope Joyce is here," Milinqua said. "It will be so much easier that way."

"Yes," Corlin said, turning slightly as she walked and glancing behind at the men who followed. Rutgers was walking quite close and moving almost as quickly as she and Milinqua, but Ford trailed well behind, his hands jammed in his pockets, his eyes firmly fixed on the ground. She did not like to have either of these men walking this close to her, but there was nothing she could do about it. Milinqua himself did not seem so bad. There was a spark of kindness about him. His friendliness seemed genuine enough. But why would August want to see him? That was the part that was hard to understand. When he had said it, it had sounded so sensible. He had said he was tired of running and hiding and she could understand that. But wouldn't they just take him away? Put him in prison or something? She thought so, but August must have known that too. So then, why?

"Do you know what strikes me about this place?" Milinqua asked, glancing toward her and smiling pleasantly. "The pureness of it, the genuine whiteness of your grass and dirt, the school rising in the distance like a palace. Have you ever comprehended how medieval your existence is here? I see your school as a castle, your creek as a circling river, and your few cottages and dormitories as the domiciles of serfs. Or is it the town where the serfs live? I think my analogy fails at both points. You live in the town, though, don't you? And I imagine you've seen very little of the world beyond. Well, truthfully, that's fine. Let me advise you: don't. Stay here as long as you are able. After the unworldly seclusion of this life, the rest of the world will seem like a truly horrible place to you. You're like a medieval monastery here. You're keeping wisdom alive in the face of dark forces running wild throughout the rest of the world."

"No," said Corlin, shaking her head.

"Well, I didn't expect you to agree with me. I imagine you think I'm criticizing you or Dr. Larkin or your work. But that's not so. I'm trying to pay you a compliment. You can't imagine how I wish I could have spent my boyhood in a place like this. My childhood was a narrow street packed tight with beggars and thieves and gamblers and whores. That's what I meant by the rest of the world being horrible. Perhaps, to me, the opposite is true, and your school is a source of fear. I hope not, but for others I know this is true. Take my assistants as an example. Take Mr. Ford in particular. He is truly afraid of you and Dr. Larkin and this school. I have heard him talk. His hatred for you runs very deep indeed."

This time, Corlin did not reply. She was tired of answering him, nodding a yes or shaking a no, making futile stabs at conversation while the moment drew closer and closer with every new step. Suddenly, she hoped Larkin was not there, that he had stayed home and slept, but she knew that wasn't likely, and even if it were true, it could not matter. The school was coming closer now, so close that she could reach out and touch it. She didn't touch it, but here was the door.

"Hey—look!"

"Stop him—hey!"

"You there—hey—come back!"

Turning with Milinqua, Corlin saw Rogirsen streaking across the grounds. Rutgers and Ford stopped shouting and raced after him. Rogirsen ran straight for the woods, and she stood, watching, until he reached the first of the trees and disappeared among them. They would not catch him in there. She knew that. But Rutgers and Ford did not. They went after him.

Milinqua said, "They won't catch him there."

Corlin said, "No."

"Well, in that case, no use poking here. They'll know where to find us. Come along."

Together, they entered the building, marching sharply down the corridor toward Larkin's office. Corlin listened to the sounds of passing classrooms, young voices lifted in learning, and she marveled at the normality of the day. It didn't seem right somehow, but she could see there really wasn't any choice. What did she expect Larkin to do? Dismiss all classes? Declare a holiday, a day of internal mourning?

Larkin was alone in the office, seated behind his desk. He looked all right to her, healthy and rested. Except for the gun and his folded hands, the top of the desk was bare. Larkin said, "I wanted to give this to you." He balanced the weapon in the palm of his hand. "I saw you coming and drew it out."

"When I leave," Milinqua said, "remind me to take it. What is it for?"

"I've had it for years. As a precaution. But I don't think it's safe. Not with the children."

"I see," Milinqua said. "Wasn't that one of your men who was just running away from us? I forget his name . . ."

"Michael Rogirsen," Corlin said.

"Yes, that's it. Tell me, Joyce, why was he running?"

"He's been transformed."

"Well, that explains it." Milinqua smiled shyly. "I'm afraid Miss McGee forgot to tell me about that. Well, that makes—how many?—seven, isn't it? Something like that. The children who were holding me captive last night—they too were caught."

"I thought so," Larkin said, sounding distracted.

"But what was odd, I barely caught a glimpse of the boy myself. Not even then, with him close enough to touch, because when he arrived, it was very late and I was nearly asleep and it was very dark inside the cabin. We had no light. Too bad, for as you can imagine, I was quite curious. Still, I soon ought to have my chance to meet him."

"Why is that? Have you found him?"

"You don't know?"

"How can I know? I haven't seen August since the first night."

"That's a pity—but it isn't significant."

"August is coming here," Corlin said. "I saw him this morning and he asked me to arrange a meeting. Tallsman is with him now."

"But why?" Larkin said.

"I think he wants to go away."

"But why here?"

"I think he intends to bring the other children with him."

"And you don't know why?"

"He didn't explain anything to me," Corlin said. "That's what makes it strange, because this morning when he told me, I didn't think anything of it. He said for me to do it and I just went ahead and did it exactly like he'd said. But now I'm not so sure. I don't know. Don't you think he has to know what he's doing? I know you haven't seen him, but he's still the same, but in other ways he's changed too. I can't understand it."

"He's only a twelve-year-old boy," Larkin said. "Maybe he's afraid."

"I don't think so," Corlin said. "I don't think anything could frighten him, because I don't think anything could harm him. Not unless he wanted it to."

Milinqua interrupted: "I can tell you this much, Joyce: If the boy does indeed come here and he surrenders himself willingly to me, then I will ensure that my final report is modified accordingly and that you receive all the credit you properly deserve. And I feel it will be best that way for everyone concerned. I don't want you to think I'm doing you a personal favor. I'm not. I simply cannot see any legitimate reason why you ought to fall needlessly into disfavor with certain important parties. Do you understand?"

Larkin said that he did. He thanked Milinqua for the favor anyway.

Milinqua had gone to the window. He stood with his hands resting against the wall, his legs spaced evenly beneath him, and his face pushed near the glass. He said, "Here are my men at last. I see we guessed correctly, Miss McGee. They are quite alone. But, well, there is really no place a man can run where we cannot find him in time. Perhaps I had better go out and reassure my men. I don't want them to think they have failed me."

He started toward the door, and Corlin said, "I think I'll stay here. If you don't mind."

"Yes," Milinqua said. "I think that would be best."

When she was alone with Larkin, Corlin stood nervously across from his desk and waited for him to speak, but he said nothing, simply returning her gaze and grinning. Then he shook his shoulders, lowered his grin, and looked at the gun he held loosely in his hand. He began tossing it easily into the air and catching it, moving cautiously, as though the gun were a fragile glass. Corlin watched, but he still said nothing, so she went to the window and looked out at the school grounds. It was definitely going to be a good day. It might even be hot. If nothing else, she was sure of the weather. The sky was clear and bare and naked like a well-scrubbed face and faraway sunlight glinted narrowly against distant trees. She kept standing and staring and waiting for him to speak, but he said nothing. The gun popped up and the gun fell down, spinning in the air. Larkin caught it by the barrel, flipped it again, let it turn once in the air and caught it. He never faltered. Not once. He watched it turning, his eyes shining bright, and she wondered why it always had to end this way. Sheridan and Tallsman and now Larkin himself. How many others to come? When would she find someone who would listen even after it was over?

"Here he comes," she said. "It's him."

She felt Larkin's presence at her side. His hand gripped her wrist. He said, "Are those the other ones? The four?"

"Yes," she said. "No—wait," she said. "One of them isn't there."

"You're right. There's only three. And August."

"One of the girls is missing. There's Steven and Lynda and Thomas."

"Milinqua has seen them."

And they both watched as the four small figures emerged from the woods and went one way while the three larger figures turned away from the school and went another way. Then all seven came together in a group between the woods and the school, near the woods. They stood close to the creek, which swept indifferently past them, and they were talking. She thought they were talking.

"I wish I knew what they were saying," she said.

"Don't you know?" His hand found her hand and squeezed tightly.

"No, I don't," she said, her hand held loose.

CHAPTER 30

GREGORY TALLSMAN:
Iron Bars and Glass Walls

The forest held tightly clinging around him now, each tree separately swaying in the breeze as though individually placed by some giant hand in such a fashion as to confirm the worst of his suspicions of unnatural confinement. Tallsman marched compliantly with the children, but his feelings were not helped by the manner in which August led the party, slipping between closely growing trees with only inches between their towering trunks, dropping to the ground and crawling beneath heavy thorn bushes that blanketed the invisible path they were following, sliding on hands and knees through mud and dirt. When they had first moved away from the cabin and into the woods, Tallsman had intended to continue his conversation with the girl Lorcas, but he had soon become far too busily involved with the dulling processes of moving relentlessly forward. He had no energy left to expend at talking. He was following the girl and she was following the boy ahead of her and the chain proceeded inexorably onward to August himself. From previous rain, the forest was damp and all of their clothing was speckled by bits of dark clinging mud. Tallsman tried his best to ignore it, for now the sun beamed precariously from one corner of the sky. It certainly looked like a good day coming. He was happy about that.

Nor did he know their final destination. He thought it un-likely that this hike was merely a hike, a walk in the early morning, a chance to see the forest as yet undisturbed by the gathering sun, so he guessed they must be heading for the school, but only because the school was the only place they could be heading. If so, why hadn't they continued along the creek and gone straight to the school that way and avoided all this crawling and sliding and slithering? And why did they want him along? Or did they? Lorcas, for one, had acted friendly and glad to see him (telling him how much she enjoyed his classes, though he could not remember ever having seen her there) but none of the others had said a word to him, and he was beginning to feel like a man stranded deeply in the bowels of some nameless foreign city surrounded by a million men but unable to communicate a simple thought to any of them. These children, whoever or whatever they had become, spies or visitors or gods of destiny, did not lessen his anxiety. And what was worse: Of them all, it was August who seemed the most genuinely human. August. Not the others, some of whom he had known and taught for years. Not even Lorcas. Once, he had known them all well; now they were strangers again.

But wait. So here it was, after all. Strange that he hadn't noticed it coming. The forest cracked and parted in front of him, exposing a green, rolling, neatly trimmed expanse of grass, which ran forward at a hurrying pace only to stop short at the brink of the distant school building. August lifted a hand and the children halted. They were still fairly well concealed. A tall hedge of untamed bushes separated the edge of the forest from the land beyond. Turning, August whispered something to Steven. Tallsman could not hear. The others nodded sharply as though they had.

While the children awaited further orders, Tallsman took a few steps to the right so that he could see through an opening in the hedge. There was someone standing out there, but he could not see clearly. No, there were two people standing out there and, as he watched, a third figure came out of the building and joined the others. Could August see them? Not with his eyes—not unless he had developed the ability to see through leaves and wood. Tallsman thought to warn him, but it was already too late. Moving forward, August pushed his way through the hedge and stepped into view. The three figures saw him, turned and approached. The children went after August. Tallsman gulped a breath of air, swept his arm forward, and caught Lorcas around the neck. She fell, and he pulled her back, then dropped above her, stifling her screams. But she wasn't screaming, he realized, and he did not move. He had recognized the approaching figures and remembered their proper names but now it was too late to warn any of the others but at least he had saved this girl. Drawing her deeper into the forest, he dropped down again, lying across her body. He could still see a wide section of the lawn. August and Steven and Lynda and Thomas continued forward. So did Milinqua and Rutgers and Ford, moving fast. Then they met.

They were standing together near the creek. Tallsman thought they were talking. Milinqua and August, they were talking. Tallsman thought it was a pleasing sight. It looked as if seven good friends had unexpectedly met on the final hole of the country club course after completing the day's round and now they were discussing their games, the heat, their wives and husbands and mutual friends. Plans were being formulated for dinner and afterward. Lying softly on the wet ground, the odor of mud in his nostrils, his hands cold and shivering, Lorcas moving to his side, her head tucked close to the ground, Tallsman watched. Near and around, the forest turned and swept, deeply still.

Then it seemed as if he could see everything. His eyes acted like a zoom lens, drawing close to the focal scene. He made a wrong turn, then another, before his eyes finally focused. There was a bare rock squatting deep in the high grass. A window flashed (too far—back up—but hadn't that been a face?) and then he found them. He saw Milinqua, then Steven (his eyes circling the scene), then Lynda, then Thomas, then Ford. Here was Rutgers's huge black glowering face. Then August, young and powerful and waiting. Then Milinqua again, seen better now, more distinctly, closer, his dark heavy eyes concealed by eyebrows as wide as a grown man's thumb, his sloping nose and inclined jaw, his brown heavy hands curling with tufts of black hair. A gun in his hand. The gun went up, the eyes went with it, moving ponderously, slowly, heavy as a big rock.

Milinqua aimed the gun and fired.

August fell.

The shot was clean. It hit him high on the forehead a fraction of an inch below his hairline.

August toppled and was dead.

Then back. Then all the children, gazing at August down on the ground. The children frozen stiff and straight and solid as a still photograph. Even Ford. Or Rutgers. For a long moment, nobody moved a muscle.

Then everything was moving and his eyes were back where they belonged. He heard himself saying: "He's dead—he killed him."

And then he was slapping Lorcas across the mouth. She was lying, or sitting, or kneeling near to him. She had not moved, so he was slapping her, holding her head straight and hitting her with the flat of one hand. As he struck her again and again, his hand burned like fire. Her mouth opened once as though she intended to speak. Blinking, she said nothing. He slapped her and pulled her. He wanted to run but he wasn't going to run alone. She spoke, so softly that he barely heard. She said, "Why? Why? He . . ."

"Come on." And he was dragging her through the woods, plowing over and between bushes, and then she was running and pulling and she fell, stumbling. She ran with tears in her eyes, saying, "Why? Why? He . . ."

Tallsman didn't know how long they ran, because the next thing he knew they were walking. They walked deep within the forest. Her clothes were torn and ripped, one long strip trailing behind and flopping like a colorful tail. He kept his hands in his pockets, thick with filth and mud, and tasted blood draining from cuts and scrapes and open wounds, blood sprinkled across his face like red raindrops, flowing between his lips and running down his throat. He tasted blood and swallowed.

They came to a tree. Tallsman looked up. The tree was very

tall. A hundred feet, two hundred, he couldn't tell. It was old too. He stepped close to it and tried to wrap his arms around the trunk but his hands missed touching by a yard or more. This was no ordinary tree; it had to be the oldest and biggest in the forest. They sat down together beneath its branches.

Lorcas leaned close to his chest and wept against him. She was crying out of grief—no, he thought, not that—what?—relief?

"I don't care if he's dead," she said, later.

"Why? I don't—"

She put her finger against his lips, then the finger opened, parted, spread, and she put her hand against his hand, and all the fingers opened, parted, spread, his fingers and her fingers just like one, and then like clay flowing gently together. Tallsman felt nothing, watching. Eight fingers were one finger. Fatter than before. A bright shiny thumb. A bent wrist, one wrist only, with blood and veins, but all the same.

She buried her face in his chest, cracking the skin, parting it, gnawing suddenly at his heart.

Then, screaming, he tried to stand, but his feet were locked in her thighs, his toes spread within her knees. Her clothes opened, gliding away from her body, exposing her skin, and then it was just the two of them. Nothing between.

Tallsman felt dirty, lying inside her.

Was he screaming now? He wanted to scream but he wasn't sure if he could. He tried again, but his mouth lay very near her eyes and he was afraid of hurting her with his teeth. So he kept his lips sealed. His own eyes saw nothing but dark interior flesh, yet her vision afforded him bright tempting glimpses of the old tree endlessly spinning, whirling, leaves fluttering like green sails in a raw wind.

So he was no longer screaming.

No use; too late; he was lost. Or—was it won?

One?

The tree wavered.

He began to sense the meaning of . . .

He thought: And on and on and on. Endlessly, he saw it. The tree was going to fall.

CHAPTER 31

CHORUS:
One of Us Will Soon Be You

So here lay the boy's poor body, lonely and awkward beneath the approaching clouds of noon. Above the lawn it was lying, and when it was eventually moved, a bare spotting depression would remain, a few crushed blades of grass in a vaguely human shape, but night would soon be falling, then passing, and dawn would then be coming, and when it came, even that would be obliterated. What would then remain as proof? A grave, perhaps, but far from here. A covered hole deep in the earth. Or more importantly, here and there, a few scattered recollections buried within the minds of a handful of men and women, boys and girls. These recollections would represent the boy's sole claim to a transient sort of immortality. Nothing else would remain.

So both the man, who was very old (Joyce Larkin), and the woman, who was considerably younger (Corlin McGee), came down from the school to gaze upon the boy's poor body. It was the old man who knelt down, moistening his hands in the thick grass, and felt the dead veins of the boy's wrist while the woman turned and gazed down the road, watching the departing motor car gliding gracefully away in the direction of the warming sun. She wished it well, now that it had gone, but to the old man she seemed strangely troubled. He did not quite understand. More at ease under these circumstances, more familiar with sudden death, he sought to reassure her.

—I wonder why he . . . (she began).

—Came here? Now I don't think . . . (he said).

—Not that he could ever have expected. Not this. But why did they kill him?

—To end it. To put a final finishing chapter on a long story. Say it however you want to say it. A man once wrote that every story has its natural end in death if you bother to carry it far enough forward. All life—everything—is actually a tragedy.

—Oh, don't be morbid. Really, Joyce. This isn't the time. We have enough to worry about. What are we going to do now? You and me and the others? Tell me that.

—I suppose we go back to teaching. And learning. Or both. That isn't morbid, is it? Go back to doing what we've always done before and doing it as well as we can. What else can I say?

—Of course. Say it. And Rogirsen? What about him? Or Melissa? The other children? Lynda and Steven and Lorcas and Thomas? What about them? Always details. Are you going to write their parents and explain? At least August had nobody except you and me.

—They're gone now. We're forgotten. Nothing has changed. Nothing ever changes except, perhaps, change itself.

—Oh no. Don't say it. Is that all you can say? Nothing changes. Why do all old men end up sounding like senile Chinese patriarchs? Does something turn rotten in the blood after eighty years?

The conversation had reached its natural end, so they turned together and went back toward the school, leaving the body where it lay, heavy with pints of useless blood, eyes wide open, skin as clean and pure and sparkling as a baby's. August was dead.

Near by, on the road between town and school, Antonio Milinqua, local area supervisor, sat scribbling hasty notes in a hand-sized spiral notebook. The car in which he was riding was exceedingly crowded, its two narrow seats, back and front, containing a total of six people. This was not so bad as it might seem, for three of these people were young children. In the front seat, a girl sat between Milinqua and Rutgers, while in the back, Ford was flanked by a pair of boys.

Ford fidgeted in his seat. He did not like having these children so close to him. And he wanted to ask Milinqua a question. He wanted to ask why he'd shot the kid. But he knew better. He wasn't going to ask that kind of question. He knew when to keep his mouth shut. Someday, this particular bit of information might be useful, and he intended to hold on to it until that day arrived.

Rutgers, meanwhile, was also curious, but he kept his thoughts deeply buried, for he was possessed of a strong and definite sense of loyalty toward his superior. He knew what Ford was thinking. He always knew what Ford was thinking as clearly as though he had uttered his thoughts aloud, but knowing Ford, knowing how he acted as well as thought, he preferred to ignore him. He expected eventually to inherit the title of local area supervisor, and he knew when he did he would feel gratified by all the years of loyalty he had given his superior, and he only hoped, when the time came, that he could find a man as true and faithful and honest as he had always tried to be.

But he wasn't quite sure why Milinqua had killed the boy. He had an idea. He thought that Milinqua had done it in order to set the other children free. He wasn't sure if that made sense. He didn't know enough about the case. But he did know that Milinqua never acted without good reasons, that he was far from a casual killer, and this was the only reason he could imagine. He carefully studied the girl who sat at his side, gazing intently at her eyes, noting the shallowness of her color and texture, the way she sat, slumped and bent and undisciplined, and the way her facial muscles seemed to hang listlessly from the wide bones beneath her skin. And he listened to the way she babbled, struggling to discern the words that lay beneath the surface of noise. He could not imagine why she was babbling this way, but Ford in the back knew it was because the dead boy's possessive spirit had relinquished control of her soul and was now speedily fleeing the physical confines of her body. Ford was a pragmatic man, who would never have spoken such a thought aloud, or even thought this way consciously, but down deep Ford was also an average man, and such a man has little conscious control over the depths of his true thoughts.

—Down in the cabin when he you remember how fully because I barely can remember sensations and feelings sharp as words are like . . . (This was the girl, babbling.)

In the beginning, the two boys had also babbled, but they had stopped after a time. Ford wished the girl would stop too. Rutgers thought: *For a child, she's actually quite intelligent. Such clear diction—and powerful words, uncommonly strong words.*

Rutgers knew that the girl and the boys would soon be out of their hands. A delegation had already come from the research installation to discuss the matter with Milinqua, and several men were presently awaiting the arrival of the children. In a few minutes, it would all be over. He didn't know what would happen to the children then, but he hoped none of them would have to die. The children were intelligent and bright. What had happened to them had been a shame. But it hadn't been their fault. And the one who had caused it was dead.

Ford thought: *I wish she'd shut her mouth.* And deep down, he thought: *A soul as long as a snake's belly, long, never ending, around and around, endlessly round.*

Milinqua said:

—The boy was resisting arrest, I believe. Yes, I seem to recall seeing him running toward the woods. That's right. And when he turned at my warning shot, I had no choice but to fire again. I hit him in the head. A bad shot. I had aimed for his knees. After that, I believe he died instantly, or at least very close to it, and that will have to do. And his body will be forwarded at the first available opportunity to the island research facility. No doubt of that.

Reaching inside his coat, Milinqua removed his gun, black and slick and shiny, and lowering the window, he poked the gun outside and fired a single shot.

He said:

—My warning shot.

Then, tucking the gun back in his coat, he grinned at the road ahead.

Rutgers grinned with him.

Rogirsen poked his head from the edge of the woods, his eyes darting furiously like circling hawks. He had never seen this many cars in his life. Where had they all come from? He had never known there were this many people living on the island. He had run and run, taking new paths through the woods, and then crossing cultivated land, where stalks of corn grew taller than a man, small well-tended gardens of corn and some vegetables, sufficient to feed a farmer and his family, and no one had seen him stopping to eat, so he had kept on running. For a time it had seemed as though entire days were passing as he ran, days without nights, and he had kept on running and running and once he had fallen, lying blank and spent, and then it had seemed as if a great weight had been lifted from his back, and when that was done, he had regained his feet and run again and come here.

Now he was trying to convince himself that nothing was wrong, but the act of running had reawakened many newly buried fears, and fear was not an easy emotion to subdue.

Waiting, struggling with his fear, he lay low, nearly flat against the earth, supporting the upper portion of his body by the elbows. The earth became for him a reminder of the land beside the creek. It smelled much the same, rich and free. There was a hint of running water in it and the bare whipping noise of passing fish. He knew there was a creek or a stream somewhere near. He would have liked to have gone home again. But he knew that was impossible.

At last, despite the fact that his fear was running as strong as ever, he made himself move away from the earth, and he began to edge toward the highway, crouched low, his fingers nearly touching the ground. Then, standing, he thrust himself full into view, with his eyes clamped shut and his muscles tightly flexed, poised to flee back to the woods. He felt the eyes of the motorists staring at him as they drove past, their huge cars tossing the wind against his face, firm as a hand's slap, and then, when he was sure he couldn't stand another second of it, a car stopped.

At first it didn't stop fully. It paused at the side of the road, and the driver looked at him through the glass.

Rogirsen watched it moving.

Then it stopped. An arm emerged from the window and waved furiously at him.

Rogirsen ran to the car.

The man said:

—Are you looking for a ride? I couldn't tell.

—Yes.

—I saw you standing here and I wondered. Nothing's wrong?

—No. I just want to go.

—Where? Town? I'm going to town. You can ride along.

—Yes, that's where I'm going. Thank you.

The man opened the rear door and Rogirsen slipped into the seat. He felt much better now, safer, muscles loose and relaxed. He was no longer afraid. The car would take care of the running for him. It moved into the traffic stream, cars whizzing past on both sides, getting dark now, the sun hidden by the trees, switching lanes and popping into open spaces. Rogirsen leaned back in the seat and watched.

—Is somebody chasing you? You're not in trouble?

—No.

—I didn't mean anything. I was only wondering. You see, back there where I found you, there's nothing there. That's why I wondered what you were doing there.

—I'd gone for a walk. In the woods.

—Oh, I see. I thought that might be it. I didn't mean anything by what I said before. Actually, to tell the truth, I sort of admire anyone who's in trouble these days. It's a good time for a man to be running. I suppose if I were younger than I am, I might be in there running too.

—I see. But I'm not running.

—Have you got a place to stay in town?

—No, I haven't. I was staying with some friends on a farm, but I thought I'd move on.

—Well, I can find you a good place to stay. There's one place I know, it's a good place. In fact, it's so good that if you were running, or somebody was chasing you, they would never be able to find you there. That's a good place, isn't it?

—It sounds like it is. Yes.

Far away, passing acres of trees and grass and ferns and vines, colors slowly dying with the end of the day, across and beyond neat cultivated farms, where corn grew higher than a man's head, near the creek, in point of fact, lay two who were like one, part of a man and part of a child, frozen naked and embracing, as still and unmoving as a single grain of sand.

The shadows of impending darkness had begun to encroach upon this silent form. Its feet were buried fully in darkness while the head, turned toward the sky, was shining clear and bright with lingering light. Above stood the tree sweeping straight toward the sun, never seeming to pause till the end of its defiant ascent, branches first sprouting halfway up the trunk, swaying lightly in the breeze, fluttering and nodding briefly. Around the tree, the air was clean and clear and fresh. A squirrel came scampering down the trunk to see, then fled, tail jerking high.

One part (the man part) was thinking:

Too late for tomorrow. What can I do? Remembering what never happened to me, seeing with eyes not my own. But there is no me, or I or mine, only an it, only this one. Man coming late into the house with a broken face, cracked as though struck by a chisel. Talking about day's papers and snow whitely blanketing the land all around. Prints drawn deeply in the snow, hands tiny and white speckled with signs of aging. Much smaller hands than yesterday. Everything, always shrinking, old man. Not mine. Mine's been taken away by the other one. Cannot remember me. No more I.

Class dismissed!

The children ran down the steps, leaving the school, though a few dallied behind in order to talk to their teachers. But most were gone, and one voice cracked, "Tallsman's not—" only to be brushed aside by, "They're not here. Not a one of them. They haven't come back."

But curiosity, unlike grief, is not a lasting emotion, so when it came time to eat, all of the children had a hearty meal, and afterward, some went down to read or study while others played fleetingly across the darkening grounds. Larkin came out and stood watching them.

—He's going to kick off before the month's out.

—No. Not him.

—There's something wrong with his guts, always holding on like he's afraid they'll spill out if he lets go.

—No. He's all right.

—He's ninety-nine and a half years old. What do you think? He can't live forever. He's got to go sometime. Why not now?

—Why should he? Why should you get to see it? My two brothers and sister all came here and they thought they were going to see him go too. He didn't go; he's still here. And he's only eighty-eight or eighty-nine.

—You see him get killed?

—I was on the other side. In a study. I'm pretty sure I heard the shots, though.

—They were loud. You couldn't have missed them. Like a cannon going off. I saw the whole thing. They were trying to keep us back from the window but I fought through and peeked. I saw it. Shot him three times in the heart and then got him twice more in the head. Shot him once in the head when he was down. His brains were splattered all over the lawn.

—They were not. I went and saw. A little blood.

—She cleaned it up.

—Well, why didn't she clean the blood too?

—Hey, look—he's coming over.

Larkin approached the children. So this was how they played tag nowadays, the lot of them laughing and talking as cool as ice water. When he was a boy, it hadn't been this way, not when you were playing serious tag. There was something important missing from the game the way these kids played it. Maybe it was the sense of quiet desperation, the wordless despair of the one who was *it*, running until exhausted or torn apart by the taunts of the others, who could never be caught. Then he turned and ran for home, screaming.

—I want you children to know everything's going to be all right. I want you to tell your friends who aren't here right now. The problem is over. The incident today, horrible as it surely was, is over now. We must try to forget it. Accept it, if you can, as something which had to happen.

—Why'd they kill him, Larkin?

—I don't know. I wish I did.

—Was he an agent of the enemy?

—That may be. Yes, that may very well be. We'll never know for certain, but we must all keep in mind that these are desperate times. Many things can happen. Almost anything.

—What about Steven and the others? Are they going to have to go into the army?

—I don't think so. I can't imagine why. I'm sure what will happen is that they will be asked some questions. When they answer and tell everything they know, they'll be sent home to their parents.

—They won't be coming back here?

—Not right away. Possibly next year. That will be up to their parents.

—They did that kidnaping. Won't anything happen to them for that?

—Well, he's decided to forgive them. He told me himself.

Inside the main school building, Corlin McGee listened to the boy who was telling her the story of his life. Her appointments were stacked as far back as yesterday morning, and she felt a driving need to put them up to date as soon as possible. Which was why she was working now. This late. Not until then, she felt, could she expect to resume the normal daily routine of her life, if that was what she actually wanted to do, and while she wasn't too sure of that, she was sure that this was as good a place as any to begin.

—Back. Back. I want to know about your own life. You as Jonathon Watson. A baby. Remember we talked of this before. Remember.

—Yes, I remember.

—What can you remember?

—I'm back and sleepy. I remember that. No, I'm sleeping. That's it—asleep. A hand, crisscrossed with wide intricate lines like a tattoo—no, more like a spider's web, a huge hand like a mountain, the pores open and draining like rivers or streams, trying to hurt, big—

—No. Go back. That was a dream. Look back at what you see.

Here was her normal daily routine. Jonathon Watson was a young boy, a first-year student, and he was just commencing his therapy. How many times had she gone through this? How many children had heard her saying these same dulling, repetitious phrases? Back and back. No, it's a dream. Look for the person. Is this what she truly meant to go on doing? Like Larkin had said, teaching and learning and maybe both. She thought of the nights with Sheridan and the weekends with his friends and the days here in the office, all of this yet to come. And what about Tallsman, off in the woods somewhere, probably asleep under a big rhododendron bush? What about him? And Larkin? What about all of them?

The boy was still talking. He was two years old and he was having a dream.

—Stop. Up. Look at me.

—Passing through a . . .

—No, come up, Jonathon. Air flows through your lungs. Taste it, breathe it. Your name is Jonathon Watson and I am Corlin McGee. You are ten years old and a student at New Morning school. Come and look at me.

—Yes. All right.

The boy glared at her. He had been having a happy time.

—What's the matter? (he asked).

—I'm sorry. I'm tired.

—But we didn't do anything. It was just those same dreams. When are we going to get to the people?

—Later. You have to know yourself, your true self, first. Didn't I tell you that?

—I guess you did. But why do we have to go over and over?

—We don't. In a week. All right? Your regular time.

She assisted him to the door, saw him free to the night, went immediately back to the office. It was time for her to be going. She had made up her mind. I'm leaving here tomorrow, she thought. If I wait a day, I'll never get out. Staring coldly at the walls which had enclosed her for so many years without her ever once having seen how much like the bars of a cage they were, she slammed her fist into her palm. Then she laughed at herself.

But where would she go? Away from this island at least.

But never mind that, she thought.

Leaving the light burning behind, she vacated the office, locking the door. The corridor swept long in front of her and she stood alone for a long moment, gazing down its entire length, deep and straight and white, like the belly of a great whale.

Late in the Pelly Tower, on the fourteenth floor, a hand was furiously scribbling notes on a sheet of white paper, aware that the computer knew this writing well enough to decipher all but the most illegible of squiggles, transforming them into words of firm substance and definite structure.

The hand (which belonged to Antonio Milinqua) was formulating a report, which tentatively read: *Suspect attempting to avoid arrest, and officer left with no alternative but to fire, or else risk escape of suspect. A warning was issued but—*

The hand scribbled a few additional words. It was easy for Milinqua to write like this. He enjoyed the chance to tell lies, and each additional word he wrote only added to his general amusement. But he was getting tired of being amused. He needed a moment for serious thinking. He dropped the pen to the desk and let his mind slide open.

(Foot burning with the pain of movement, crawling now across the burning floor, where bare splinters attack the exposed flesh like the glistening barbs of disturbed wasps, and the thing, mere yards away, is coming apart, evenly divisible into its two original components, splitting like the two pasted halves of a rubber toy. Oh hurry, he screams, not now, not me, but the thing is whole and coming toward him, the thing is itself and moving calmly across the flames like a lion stalking its prey, a face as clean and unmarked as any boy's, but it is a boy, he thinks, only a boy of twelve, now looming down, now touching, now flesh slipping inside flesh, clothes unfurling like a cloth tossed to the wind—)

Milinqua dropped a shutter across his thoughts. He wiped his brow. His hands were wet. Perhaps it was a hot night tonight; it wasn't that hot. Returning to the report, he scribbled hurriedly, letting the words of amusement blot the furious thoughts from his mind. He wrote: *Body has been removed from resting place and will be enclosed with this report upon submission to proper headquarters. Dr. Joyce Larkin, founder and owner of school, whose invaluable assistance in this matter—*

Laughing aloud, he felt ashamed. Well, it was better laughing than remembering. The horror of the murder had been nothing compared to the terror of the cabin. He could think about the murder all day, but the cabin was something he would have given his life to have wiped from his memory. He knew transformation was a wonderful thing. He knew that now, but he had not known when it happened. He had been afraid, more truly afraid than at any time in his life. He had never feared death, for death was merely a release from life, while this other thing, this thing crawling toward him on the floor, seemed far worse, a rushing toward life, and it was this that he had feared.

But it was all right now; it was safe now; he was an enlightened being now.

Though he had slain his Messiah. He thought: *I am Judas; But I shall also be Paul.*

He couldn't see where he had had any choice. If events had been left in the hands of the boy, the chemically created Messiah, the Christ of the scientific age, the end would never have been in doubt. He knew the kind of men who ruled this world. They were not of the type to allow a being like August to live. What they had created, they would also destroy, and they would have hunted him down, and his converts as well, and exterminated the lot as casually as a cat kills a mouse. No, not like a cat kills a mouse. That was an obsolescent simile. Like a soldier killing another soldier. Hunting each one down, child or man, and killing him in the cold, impersonal fashion of a soldier on the battlefield. Milinqua was certain of this, for he would have been one of those assigned to do the hunting and killing.

But then his own conversion had occurred, most ironically, as if Pontius Pilate had been made to believe in the Christian god, but when it was done and too late, he had seen the answer in a way no child, human or otherwise, could have seen it. He was writing this report and it was amusing him to tell lies, but more than that, this report was their salvation. Here was their guarantee of continuing life. All of them, except the one, except August, who was already dead, slain at the hand of the one man who had been able to convince him of his own sincerity in exposing a path to salvation. Come to me and I will ensure that you will not have to run and hide any longer. Isn't this what you want? I am your convert, your disciple, and you may surely put your faith in my hands. And then killed him. Without his ever guessing the truth until it was much too late.

What had he been, after all? The Messiah? Or merely some mock replica of a human being possessing more in common with those low-born creatures who multiply microscopically by absorbing their own brothers and sisters? Wasn't this all that August had been? Was his murder any greater sin than coughing into the palm of one's hand and slaying a million bacteria in the process?

(Squeezing the trigger, fist slamming into his side, imploding deeply, and he bites his lip, screaming so as not to scream, and sees Rutgers seeing and wipes his mind clean so that he will forget, scrubbed and blank and empty, and the echoing screams of the others slice deep, engraved forever in his memory.)

He wrote more, again using the words to smother his thoughts: —*was absolutely essential to the successful termination of the case and whose loyalty to the present establishment, despite his occasionally irregular beliefs, can not be presently doubted.*

Enough. Again, he dropped the pen and his mind slipped open, but this time he steered it away from recollection and turned instead reaching outward to touch those others, so that they would know and he would know that none of them were ever truly alone.

(Melissa: A cold room, walls rippling with ice. Sanitary, sparkling instruments, slicing and probing. Man says we only want to find out if— All men saying this but she is under again and unable to avoid this singularly crucial moment of her life, but she is happy this way, satisfied to live and relive this one moment, over and over again. Why can't you talk? You ought to be able to talk. You must tell us. We have to know— But she has nothing to say to them. Her face burns fiercely with nova-like splendor, igniting the ice in this cold room. A pity that none will ever know why.)

(The three: A moving car, open wide to the night. Men whose lips are sealed as tightly as a double-locked door. Uncaring of the when and why and where and who, undemanding men who are only messengers and not concerned beyond that point. They drive, carrying these three children, two boys and a girl, and they are not even surprised by the fact that the children, no longer requiring the bare rudiments of personality, seem no more unalike than three identical kittens from the same litter. Chattering furiously among themselves, not quite babbling now, saying only that which is necessary to stifle the horrible truth of the head blowing, exploding, cascading. Dead. *Oh why?* the children inwardly scream. But—why not?)

(Rogirsen: In a most precious place. This old boardinghouse packed with people four and five to a single room, most of them young and considering him an outlaw like themselves. They speak softly of elsewhere, and Rogirsen thinks of the enemy, yet he is aware that none of them think this way. Elsewhere, a place where a man can truly be free, but he cannot rid himself of his friend's dying self. A girl comes to his room and speaks gently to him, her questions abruptly probing for exposed tissue while her gentleness remains draped above her curiosity. But this is better, he reminds himself, answering. This is the beginning.)

(Lorcas: Who lies now opening, eyes swirling, seeing, done with minds of thinking teaching talking. Black is the sky winkly blinkly stars. And the moon. It must be night, she realizes.)

(Tallsman: Who awakes. And is.)

Him too now, Milinqua thought. Tallsman. Another mature man with whom he must speak, confide, confess, but not until after he has proved his ability to withstand the initial shock of awakening, that he is strong enough to bear the burden of an enlightened self without folding weakly under.

An enlightened self?

Melinqua shook his head. He found it hard to believe that such a term applied. Transformation was merely being allowed to see with the eyes of another, hear with another's ears, feel with his nerves, and think with his brain.

But was this enough to turn a man into an enlightened being?

Or merely a human being? Especially human? Truly human? Or simply human?

Milinqua drew the pen and paper toward him and wrote again with furious, hasty scribbles.

CHAPTER 32

STEPHANIE MILLGATE TALLSMAN:
When Is This Time Called Now?

They lay like angels sleeping, she thought. But hadn't every woman since the dawn of time thought that? Every mother? Even the heavy ape-like cave woman rocking on broad stocky legs, staring into the darkened rear of her home, where her children slept, flames casting tall fearful shadows against stone walls, and her mate prowling near the mouth of the cave, thought: *They lay like angels sleeping.* Or had there been any angels then? Maybe just spirits. Children of the fire and rain. The river and the mountain. The sun and the moon. But my children—thought Stephanie—they lay like angels sleeping.

Now there was a chance to rest. The door shut and the feet pattered toward the folds of the chair, which held her like the warmth of spring, and sighing, legs freed from the strain of day's time, withdrawn and naked. Would she be seeing him again soon? Or (when) ever? The children slept so soundly now. Well, they were older now. When they were younger, she remembered, neither had slept very well. Stanley was the worst. It was a fine day when he slept five hours without once waking and crying. "Nightmares," the doctor said. Had he gone away with her? Where were they sleeping? Or did they? This morning, she had seen them together. Very young, pretty, not beautiful. A voice which seemed softer than music. Well, she had probably never been angry. Or afraid. Weren't things like that beyond her life? There wasn't any reason for it. She had a good life, sitting all day, just sitting, in that office and going about that place and talking to that old man. Now Gregory. Once he had awakened in the night and cried. But no one had heard him crying. He had fallen and cut his mouth. Gregory had been gone that night. It had been a night a very long time ago. He had been only eighteen, nineteen, twenty months—eleven-thirty now. Ought to sleep for morning. Ought to do that now. How afraid she was for his returning.

There was enough light. Turn this one down soft and let the night have the room, reserving this single spot of light here by the chair. The beauty of night (even indoors) was the fact that it was always darker than day. Oh, he would have gloried in that one. He said Stephanie's proverbs. Stephanie says: Wonder of night is that it is darker than day. He said she said more common things in a more uncommon fashion than anyone since Lao-tse? Who's he? Look it up. Once she said (having seen the dawn when they were both young, childless, good friends): I never knew it did that. Never knew what? Never knew the sun rose? Well, I knew it did that, but I never knew it did that quite like that. Like what? Like popping over the horizon. Like the way a ball pops silently from the bottom of a tub of water. Stephanie says: The sun pops into the dawning sky, forcefully yet silently, like a ball pops from a tub of water.

Would she see him again? She must proceed on the theory that she would not. What now, then? Work? Or would she be able to convince them to help her? Assistance? Well, no matter. Could they force him to come back to her? There must be a regulation which said. Well, wasn't it desertion, or would they only say for him to support the children? She didn't care about that. There must be something somewhere which said. Maybe he would get bored with her. She was young and soft and pretty. Maybe she would get bored with him.

Just sitting with propped feet, not moving. When the eyes were closed, then everything was black. Another Stephanie. Some men like police or spies here this morning. Some others there. They killed him, but he was a spy. Were they gone now?

She knew she could never forgive him everything, but if he were to come back now and offer her another chance, she would forgive him everything.

What would living be worth alone, without him? It sounded strange, just thinking back, because she did not love him. So what was that? Didn't she want him and need him? What was love?

Pressing the twelve. She felt the encroaching shadows of the hour. Midnight coming near. Well, come on then, passing, and if you looked, it passed, and if you didn't look, it passed, and if you died, it still passed, going by and by. If only she could wrap a wet cold washcloth around her brain and never have to think again. How softly wet that crucial cloth upon the thinking brain. Ah stop it.

Come back to me. I know you're coming, hearing your steps as the car leaves the gates of the school. It's you who's driving down the dirty muddy road.

But that was yesterday. And before.

Can it be? That scraping shuffling sound of feet or knees upon the wood. It has to be. Back—no—door opening—no—oh hello. What can I say? Say nothing, if you wish. Not a single word? No. Oh yes standing crossing saying not a word aren't your clothes torn? There is dirt clinging to your eyes can you see and Greg your eyes are bleeding where have you been?

No don't speak. I will not speak. We have nothing to speak when you are bleeding me this way holding. This is fine with me no need to speak to me your eyes are mine. The children both are sleeping. Remember when they used to—no I will not speak. Midnight is emerging and dawn is when they will awaken. I know this is fine. Your arm is lying inside my arm just one arm now. I am not afraid. Should I be afraid? This is funny because I don't know. Lying down now. Oh please I think you should reach way down way deep inside me please. Can you feel me as I've been thinking I can feel you. Yes I think I am one with you. Yes I am sure you are fine with me. Twelve coming past us with a shudder. No I will not speak. I want to think as you are thinking now. Almost. So very near. Seconds now. I can hear it coming pounding near with you. The children are softly crying now. Someone is crying now. That's me who's crying softly now isn't it.